Phyllis Hastings was born in Bristol and can trace her West Country ancestry back about 250 years. As a child she showed great talent for ballet, but this was subsequently overshadowed by her love of writing. At eight she began writing verse and when she was sixteen had a poem on reincarnation published. Between 1935 and the outbreak of World War II she had about 450 short stories published all over the world, but it was not until after the war that she began to write full-length novels. Since then she has written over twenty novels.

Phyllis Hastings lives in Sussex.

BLACKBERRY SUMMER

Debbie converted a wing of the old farmhouse into an Academy for Young Ladies. She hoped this would enable her to make provision for her children's future careers. But she could not foresee the disastrous fire or the regret and guilt she would feel for giving her youngest son to be reared by her twin sister Dolly. Next to the farm, Dolly's wealthy husband Christopher built an imposing mansion in the Gothic style, and planned to run a racing stable, but his schemes were doomed to end in tragedy.

Books by Phyllis Hastings
Published by The House of Ulverscroft:

THE SWAN RIVER STORY
SANDALS FOR MY FEET
THE STARS ARE MY CHILDREN
HOUSE OF THE TWELVE CAESARS

PHYLLIS HASTINGS

BLACKBERRY SUMMER

Complete and Unabridged

ULVERSCROFT
Leicester

First published in Great Britain in 1982 by
Robert Hale Limited
London

First Large Print Edition
published 1999
by arrangement with
Robert Hale Limited
London

British Library CIP Data

Hastings, Phyllis, *1904* –
   Blackberry summer.—Large print ed.—
   Ulverscroft large print series: general fiction
   1. Large type books
   I. Title
   823.9'14 [F]

   ISBN 0–7089–4073–0

Published by
F. A. Thorpe (Publishing) Ltd.
Anstey, Leicestershire

Set by Words & Graphics Ltd.
Anstey, Leicestershire
Printed and bound in Great Britain by
T. J. International Ltd., Padstow, Cornwall

This book is printed on acid-free paper

Part One

Part One

1

How calm and quiet a delight
  It is alone
To read, and meditate, and write.
                    Charles Cotton

The lady stopped her carriage and pointed out the house. 'This,' she said, 'is the home of Benjamin Joseph Elphick.'

Her niece favoured it with a casual glance. 'Who is he?'

The lady was slightly shocked. Did young girls learn nothing nowadays? 'He is considered to be one of our best writers on natural history, and his illustrations are exquisite.'

'What does he draw?'

'Flowers, birds, everything that moves or blossoms.'

The niece yawned. 'I prefer pictures of people, the kind that Mr Burne-Jones paints, such as King Cophetua and the Beggar-maid.' She wished her aunt would tell the coachman to drive on. This place was nothing to make a song about, just a rambling old farmhouse whose window-frames had not seen a paint-brush for years. 'It doesn't look as though he earns much money,' she observed.

'Money is not everything,' her aunt told her, sharply. 'Probably he is not so wealthy as the authors of those cheap novelettes you read. All the same — '

But the niece had ceased to listen and, if in the future she should hear mentioned the name of Benjamin Joseph Elphick, she certainly would not connect it with the house called Marlipins.

Had Joe-Ben known that strangers occasionally stopped outside his door he would have been astonished and amused. Surely, he would have thought, pilgrimages were made only to the abode of genius, and of dead genius at that. He was merely a man who delighted in making books about the things he saw, and he was still overwhelmed when his publishers sent him money for those books. It was somehow excessive that he should be paid for so much enjoyment.

Not that the money was unwelcome. Marlipins had changed considerably over the past decade or so. It was at one and the same time more prosperous and more costly to run, and sometimes Joe-Ben would scratch his head and wonder whether they really were financially better off than in the days when, after their grandfather's death, he and his young brother Rose had struggled desperately to prevent the farm from becoming bankrupt.

He felt a certain nostalgia for the past. It was a sign of growing old, he supposed, though forty could scarcely be termed elderly. But, despite vicissitudes, there had been magic in those years, those long hours on the wide, bird-haunted spaces of Pevensey marshes, those impassioned moments when Joan had appeared like a spirit of the trees, to madden and gladden him. Now she was long in her grave, and her daughter was growing up, and nothing and no-one could take Joan's place.

More than anyone else, perhaps, could his mother have understood his feelings, had he mentioned them to her. Alice knew she had much for which to be thankful. Once she had wished the empty echoing rooms of Marlipins could be filled. Well, her wish had come true. There was now not a corner of the house which was not occupied, not a moment free from the sound of voices. Large as the family had become, there was a suite allocated to Rose's doctor wife for her surgery, and a whole wing was necessary for Debbie's school.

Sometimes, when she was particularly

tired, Alice would reflect that wishes were dangerous, because they could come true. Then she would scold herself for ingratitude. Was there anything more wonderful than to be surrounded by loving children and grandchildren? Never need she be lonely, widow though she was. That was when a pang of guilt went through her. Edmund's death had touched her so faintly. She should have mourned him more deeply, despite the years when he had deserted her. But she scarcely noticed his absence, partly because she had no time for such a luxury.

Debbie had said to her, 'Now you can sit back, mother. Just rest. You have Joe-Ben and Rose and Tirell and me, to say nothing of the children. We'll look after you.'

The prospect was one of sunshine. Unfortunately, though, resting was a habit Alice had not acquired, and even if she had, she thought, with an inward smile, she doubted she could have practised it. There were so many people requiring so many things to be done. 'It won't take more than a minute,' they assured her, which was true, but the minutes stretched to hours, and the hours to days, and so the years passed.

Everyone had expected Joe-Ben to re-marry, and there had been expectation among several local girls, who did their best to become friendly with Debbie and Tirell, and even took little presents to Alice. 'He is so handsome,' the girls sighed. 'And so eligible,' their mothers added. It seemed a shame that an attractive man who was also a celebrity should go to waste.

When their efforts were unavailing they consoled themselves, if consolation it could be called, by deciding that Joe-Ben's devotion must be centred on his daughter. It was natural, wasn't it, that a man should see his lost love in the child she had borne?

Alice knew the truth. He had shown no interest in the baby, had carelessly asked her to choose a name for it, and she, coming upon an early daisy, had settled on the flower. Little changed as Daisy grew up. It was as if Joe-Ben could never forget that his daughter cost his wife her life. It was cruel to blame the innocent, Alice knew, but she realised how much Joe-Ben suffered, and she suffered with him, for he was still her first-born, her darling miracle.

2

One step and then another,
  And the longest walk is ended;
One stitch and then another,
  And the largest rent is mended.

Anon.

Looking back over the past thirteen years of her widowhood, which she rarely desired or had the opportunity to do, Debbie was struck by the speed with which they had passed. As far as large issues were concerned they had been uneventful. 'Like a mill-pond,' she said to herself, then shivered, remembering Ninian's death.

Putting aside that tragedy, however, she felt considerable satisfaction in that alone she had raised and educated five of her six children, made a success of her own life and set them on the same road.

When she had told her mother of her plans, Alice had been shocked and terrified. 'A school? How can you? You're not qualified.'

'If you mean I have no degrees, that is true. But I am not ignorant. Wasn't

Ninian my teacher? And I can educate myself further.'

'There's the village school. We don't need another.'

'Mine will be different. I shall take boarders.'

Her mother's eyes, Debbie thought, looked as though they might pop out with amazement. 'And where would you do a thing like that?'

'Here at Marlipins. Now that Tirell has married Rose and repaid the mortgage, we need have no fear that Christopher could take possession of the place. Oh, mother, don't stare at me in that way! I'm not proposing to run a brothel.'

'Debbie! I won't have you using such language. Anyway, the house is not large enough.'

'Once you complained it was too spacious.'

'That was before Tirell had her surgery, and before you and your children — '

'We'll leave at once, if you begrudge us house-room.'

'Now, Debbie, there's no need to be so masterful.'

But Debbie was put out, for she was still filled with bitterness that she had allowed Christopher to adopt her youngest. She had tried to persuade herself that her wealthy brother-in-law would offer the child better

9

prospects than she could hope to do, but in her heart she knew that it was because young Ninian was posthumous and because he would always remind her of being raped by Christopher in his drunken frenzy.

Well, that was a long time ago. Alice had come round to accepting the school, especially after Debbie explained that the pupils would sleep in dormitories. 'I'll need only two. I'm not expecting to house a regiment. Then there must be two school-rooms and a dining-room. Five rooms in all. I don't see why I shouldn't have that east wing. You've never furnished it.'

'I've never furnished any part,' Alice reminded her, almost with pride. 'Your grandfather did what was necessary. Anyway, Rose uses some of those rooms for storage.'

'Then he must take away his things and put them where they belong, in the farm buildings,' Debbie said, briskly.

Her mother was still doubtful. 'When Christopher adopted Ninian he did offer a free cottage for you and the children, but you were too proud to take it. Wouldn't it be better — '

'No, it would not. A cottage! I want to run a school for the daughters of gentlemen.'

'But the cost! It all needs re-decorating, and that roof leaks.'

'I believe Tirell will help me.'

Alice felt a pang of pity for her daughter-in-law. 'She works so hard, and people don't expect to pay their doctors promptly, if at all. She's a rare good soul, is Tirell, and I reckon as we impose on her.'

'Rose may,' Debbie said, somewhat coldly, 'but I am only asking for a loan.'

When she looked back, she was surprised at her — well, one could call it courage, but she supposed it was temerity. It had been a struggle, and many a time the whole project had trembled on the edge of failure, but somehow she kept going, and now, with most of her children grown up and independent, she was conscious of a certain feeling of security.

Some of her ideas had caused considerable amusement among the family. 'Domestic work?' Tirell asked, with a professional woman's scorn for manual labour. 'I believed your school to be for gentlefolk.'

'So it will be, but domestic knowledge and intellectual culture should go hand-in-hand, not be antagonistic.' Debbie spoke defensively, because at that time she was not sure of herself, though she held her theories with sincerity. 'When my pupils become wives they must know how to train their servants, which they can only do adequately

11

when they themselves are able to perform the work.'

Her mother gave a sigh of relief. 'At least I'll not be flummoxed with strangers poking around, turning my home all hugger-mugger.'

'You'll not be interfered with,' Debbie assured her, 'but I'll need to engage a kitchen-maid. There are some jobs a young lady would not wish to do.'

At first she found there were many jobs at which the girls turned up their little noses. Several parents declared that they objected to paying fees for their daughters to waste their time doing housework.

'Carrying away their own bath-water. Actually black-leading grates! My child has never done such a thing, nor will she ever need to do it.'

Bravely facing irate mothers or fathers, Debbie explained the purpose of such training, though her words seemed to fall on deaf ears. Two pupils were removed from the school at an instant's notice, and no new applications for admission were received. Matters had reached so low an ebb that Debbie could see no alternative to closing what she had termed, ambitiously, her 'academy.'

'What can I do?' she asked Tirell, in

despair. 'How can I provide for my children? As you know, Bertram wants to be a doctor. How can we live? What are my qualifications? A knowledge of literature. Who wants that? A certain proficiency with figures. I suppose I could get a job in a shop at Brighton, as cashier, for ten shillings a week. How far would that go towards feeding six persons? We are parasites. We batten upon you and Rose and Mother and Joe-Ben. You make slaves of yourselves to keep us.'

'Oh, Debbie, you exaggerate. You are overtired and distracted by worry.'

Debbie burst into tears, so rare an occurrence that Tirell became really concerned.

'No-one could have made greater efforts than you have,' she assured her sister-in-law. 'I am sure this is only a temporary set-back, and after all there is only one complaint the parents make.' She hesitated, and then continued, 'Debbie, would it not be better if you engaged one or two servants? Some people do feel it is degrading for their daughters to perform menial work.'

Debbie dried her eyes. 'I have thought about it,' she confessed, 'and estimated the cost, and I really cannot afford it. There would not only be the girls' wages, but their food and uniform and a room and beds for their sleeping.'

'Then may I make a suggestion? It is a very small thing, but it might help.'

Debbie waited. 'Well? What is it? Are you afraid I might be offended?'

Tirell smiled. 'Ah! You have guessed. How quick you are! And it's true you don't always take kindly to advice. I was merely about to suggest that you take down the list of instructions posted on the wall of the dormitories.'

'How to Clean Bedrooms?'

'Yes. You have twelve items, from stripping the clothes from the beds to cleaning the windows. It frightens the girls.'

'I don't see why it should. They are here to learn.'

'Yes, but if you told them verbally, one thing at a time. Even horses have to be broken in gently.'

Debbie would not admit herself convinced, but she thought about it, and tried the experiment of putting less emphasis on domestic work. This necessitated recruiting assistance from her elder daughters. They complained, more or less bitterly according to their temperaments, but she was able to satisfy them that the extra labour was necessary. 'We depend on your grandmother and your uncles for the food we eat and the roof over our heads. If I make a success of this school you will be able to train for whatever profession you choose. In that way you will earn your own liberty. If you do not help me we may have to close the school, and then you will be poor orphans with a bleak future.'

'What kind of future?' Constance asked, her curiosity roused.

'From the present state of your school work,' their mother said, bluntly, 'you would scarcely qualify for the higher grade of governess. I would say nursery-governess at the most.'

Elianor shuddered. She was thirteen at that time, with romantic ambitions. 'I'll help,' she promised. 'I'll even wash the sides of the stairs with cold tea-water.'

'The girls will look down on us,' Constance grumbled, 'they will think we are no better than servants.'

'God will look down on you and know who you are.' As this consolation did not lighten the expression on their faces, Debbie said, 'The pupils will all know you are the daughters of the head-mistress,' and added, briskly, 'I'll see to that.'

There was no dramatic change, but gradually, as years passed, the Marlipins Academy built up the reputation of being a reliable and inexpensive country school. It did not confer any educational kudos, for the only examinations held were those Debbie herself set at the end of each term, but few parents required their daughters to be bluestockings, and, in any case, for those who could afford them, there were plenty of good finishing schools.

It was not difficult, mothers found, to paint a certain snobbish halo around Marlipins Academy.

'It is so healthy. My little girl's chest trouble has entirely disappeared. Well, they have their own farm attached to the school. Milk fresh from the cows. And cream. Lots of cream. Yes, and not only that. They have a resident doctor, living in. One could scarcely ask for more care. Standard of education? Oh, I suppose it's the same as at most schools. My little girl reads and writes very well. What more can one expect? We don't want her to ruin her eyes with a lot of book-learning. No need for it. She's as pretty as a picture. She'll marry young.'

Gradually, almost imperceptibly, the school began to prosper, until it acquired its maximum number of pupils. Debbie could not remember exactly when she wrote the first name on her waiting-list, but she well remembered the warm glow it gave her, and the feeling of having a weight lifted from her shoulders.

3

I in mine own house am an emperor
And will defend what's mine.

Philip Massinger.

Two memorable events in Christopher Waldron's life happened very close together. One was the return of his wife, together with her son, and the other was the visit of Debbie, also carrying a man-child to become a part of the Waldron household.

Remembering that thirteen-year-old agonising decision she had had to make, Debbie could still feel a soreness as of an open wound.

Before handing over the child she had found it necessary to speak privately with Dolly, and as the twins looked at one another there moved within them memories of their childhood attachment, and regret that they had grown apart.

Dutifully they began by admiring the babies, expressing polite approval, while each reflected that her own was much healthier, more prepossessing and an altogether superior specimen.

'I don't know how you can bear to part

with him,' Dolly said.

This was before Debbie had considered opening her school. 'I don't know how I shall manage,' she had confessed. 'To be left with six children and no money! If I have to go out to work — '

'But this one,' Dolly persisted, 'Your last gift from Ninian. Surely in memory of him — Why not one of the others?'

Debbie tried to keep her expression from changing, tried to keep bitterness and anger from showing. An impulse to reveal her secret was strong in her. She longed to say, 'Ninian's gift? How do I know? Your husband raped me. How can I ever be sure?' But such a disclosure would only cause pain to everyone.

She forced herself to smile. 'Christopher wants a companion for your Benjy, doesn't he? My other children are too old. He and Ninian will be almost like twins.'

'Yes. Only ten week's difference in age.'

Debbie put out her hand, touched her sister on the shoulder. 'Dolly, you will be good to him, won't you?'

Once they would have thrown their arms about one another, found strength and solace in the embrace and in a few tears, but easiness had left them and they were both embarrassed.

'I shall treat him as if he were my own,' Dolly said. Even as she spoke she realised the words had come too glibly, and she was not sure that they were true.

Debbie had stubbornly refused to allow legal adoption, and Christopher had been forced to comply, for fear she might refuse to let him have the boy. All he could do was to engage a reliable nurse for the children and instruct her to keep away from Marlipins.

The day his solicitor informed him that the mortgage he held on Marlipins had been repaid in full was so great a blow that it wellnigh robbed him of his pleasure in having the two boys.

Infuriated, he went to Dolly. 'What d'you think your scoundrel of a brother has done now?'

She looked at him inquiringly. 'Which one?'

'Rose, of course. He has sneaked off, married that doctor woman and repaid the mortgage.'

'Oh, how nice!'

'Nice? It's artful, underhand, double-dealing.'

'I meant it's nice for them to be married.'

'Convenient!' Christopher sneered. 'Easy to see why he's done it. She's got a bit of money. No, he's no fool is your brother, when it comes to playing the hand to his own advantage. You know I set my heart on Marlipins. After all, it is my family seat.'

Dolly dared to contradict him. 'Not really it isn't. Your grandfather went bankrupt and sold it to my grandfather.'

Christopher advanced threateningly towards her, and involuntarily she flinched, remembering his past violence. 'Yes, and he emigrated to Australia where my father made a fortune. Reckon it's still my home, and I need it more than ever now, for my sons.'

'They are not your sons.' Dolly spoke without thinking, and then wished she had not. 'If you hurt me,' she added quickly, 'I shall leave and take Benjy with me, and you can be sure Debbie wouldn't let you keep Ninian without me.'

Christopher recognised stalemate when he saw it, and restrained himself. One day, he thought, one day he'd get even with the lot of them. Aloud, he said, 'Don't ever again tell me Benjy is not my son. And Debbie's boy is not to be called Ninian. He is Thomas, after my father. Benjy and Tom. Understand?'

To console himself for his disappointment over Marlipins — temporary, he insisted — he embarked upon a project which was to last him several years. Without a word to Dolly, he evicted the last of the

Farncombes from the farm he had bought next to Marlipins, and proceeded to have the old house demolished.

Naturally Dolly soon heard the news. 'What are you doing to Farncombes?'

'Pulling it down, as no doubt you are well aware. Brambleden doesn't need newspapers. Every one of the inhabitants shouts the news from the rooftops.'

'But why? Why are you doing it?'

'To build a suitable house for us.'

'Oh, no! This is my home. I am used to it. I like it.'

'In the High Street, stuck between the pub and the lawyer?'

'It's a beautiful Queen Anne house.'

'Well, Queen Anne's dead. I'll sell this as soon as the other place is ready.'

'What will it be like,' she asked, timidly, 'the new house?'

'Suitable, like I said. You should be pleased, to be so near Marlipins.'

She was troubled and uncertain, but she reflected that it was impossible to move Christopher once he got a bee in his bonnet.

But though she knew him, she had no conception of what he proposed to do. He engaged a veritable regiment of workmen who spent the first three months building huts to house themselves. They were followed by teams of horses drawing waggons filled with massive stones. It took the best part of a year collecting these and laying the foundations. A group of architects was in constant attendance, and under their direction the workmen then began to erect what the local people in a mingling of derision and awe designated 'The Castle,' and would continue to do so.

It was a heavy, ornate building with enormous elaborate windows and castellated towers, the kind of edifice which in future times would be termed, somewhat contemptuously, 'Victorian Gothic.'

While this work was in progress, the grounds were being laid out by expensive landscape gardeners who rarely had so free a hand and so much room in which to work. The spacious drive could have accommodated a Royal procession, and the central fountain in front of the house could have borne comparison with any of those in the capital cities of Europe.

Two and a half years passed before the Waldrons were able to move into their new residence, and the workmen's huts remained for another six months, so many items had still to be completed.

Only one memento of the old farm did Christopher retain — its name. 'Farncombes it's been for three generations,' he said, 'so we'll keep it.'

'What do you care about the Farncombes?' Dolly asked, scornfully.

'Nothing, but I believe in upholding the ancient traditions.'

He sounded so pompous that Dolly could not resist observing, 'Quite the English gentleman.'

She thought he might turn on her in anger, but he took the remark as a compliment.

'That is what I am, and what my sons will be.'

He had not succeeded in persuading Debbie to give him legal powers over her boy, but he acted as though she had, referring to both children as his sons, except occasionally when he considered it politic to enlarge, 'Benjy is my son, and Tom is my adopted son.'

As soon as the boys were in his care he had put down their names for entering Eton College, and had arranged that when they were eight years old they should be sent away to an expensive preparatory school.

'Why must they be boarders?' Dolly asked.

'Because there is no suitable school near here.'

'There must be.'

'If they are to go to Eton — '

'I don't see why they should. Who are we that we should send them among aristocrats, titled people? They'll feel out of place.'

'We are gentry, that's what we are, and my sons will never be out of place anywhere.'

'Oh, stop calling them your sons!' Dolly exclaimed, crossly. 'We are alone, so you don't have to pretend.'

She was becoming shrewish, Christopher decided. He could still make her obey him. Oh, yes, he saw to that! But he couldn't control her tongue. Still, what could he expect? Those Elphicks had been a thorn in his side ever since he walked into Marlipins to be confronted by cussed old Benjamin. Ungrateful, that's what they were. He had given Dolly everything she wanted, built her a mansion, surrounded her with luxury.

Dolly found the new house unfriendly and oppressive, and after the boys had been sent away to school it was far worse. She would watch Christopher strutting around his estate, 'like a dung-hill cock,' she thought, and the sight made her feel sick. She had taken for herself a small room on the top floor of the house, next to the range of servants' bedrooms, and there she would retire. It had a wide view of the formal gardens, and the artificial lake and the orchards beyond. If she looked carefully, she reflected, with bitter humour, she could even catch a glimpse of one of the few remaining Farncombe fields.

'Typical of you,' Christopher sneered, 'to use a servant's room. Is that what you feel yourself to be, a servant?'

'Sometimes I wish I were,' Dolly flashed. 'At least I would have an honest job to do.'

That was the worst of it, the loneliness and the idleness. She would think of Marlipins buzzing like a hive, Tirell at one end healing people, and Debbie at the other educating children. It was good, she supposed, to have security, to know that for the rest of her life she would never want for an appetising meal, never want for an elegant gown with a rustling silk petticoat underneath. But, oh, God, how boring it was!

4

Good luck is the gayest of all gay girls;
Long in one place she will not stay:
Back from your brow she strokes the curls,
Kisses you quick and flies away.
    '*Good and Bad Luck.*' *John Hay.*

Every day since Ninian's death Debbie had thanked God for her children. Though it had been a struggle to provide for them, they had supplied her with a purpose for living and working. Now with Bertram her eldest son twenty-three years old, and her youngest daughter seventeen, she felt she could allow herself a certain satisfaction and a sense of accomplishment.

Bertram had finished his medical training and as a fully-fledged doctor was assisting Tirell in her practice.

'Is he clever?' Debbie asked, anxiously. Then, fearing this might sound like maternal arrogance, added, 'I mean, he is good at his work, isn't he? He is efficient?'

Tirell smiled. 'He is dedicated. If I had had a son — '

'You still may have.'

26

Tirell shook her head.

'As a doctor — '

'As a doctor I have to face reality. I cannot deceive myself.'

'Christopher was worried that Dolly might be — ' Debbie broke off.

'Barren? I'm not afraid of the word. That is what I am. But twins — there's a lot of superstition about them. You disproved it, though. You and Dolly were both able to bear children. For myself I have few regrets. I have my career. It is Rose I pity. He should have had sons, strong sons. Every farmer needs them.'

'Oh, Tirell, don't fret or blame yourself. Rose is happy. You have brought him so much.'

Tirell made a slight grimace. 'Just money, no more. Money to repay the mortgage.'

'And that was our life-line,' Debbie declared. 'Without it we should have lost Marlipins. I wouldn't have had the school. Mother would have broken her heart. We can never repay you for what you have done.'

'Oh, dear, how serious we are!' Tirell spoke lightly. 'Why do people become so solemn when they talk about money? But you have forgotten one thing. You should have said that you all love me for myself alone.'

27

Debbie burst out laughing. 'Indeed we do! And how should we manage without your sense of humour? You brighten the darkest day.'

'I hope so. A gloomy doctor buries more patients than a cheerful one.'

'Do you think that in time you might make Bertram your partner?'

'If he wishes it. To return to the subject of money, however, he won't make a fortune from a country practice like this.'

'I don't think Bertram cares much for money.'

Debbie was right. Yet her son's ambitions lay in a direction she had not imagined. He came to her one day with the news that he was to go to India as a medical missionary.

So shocked and astonished was Debbie that she could not think what to say. She remembered Bertram in church, bored, drawing on the fly-leaves of his prayer-book, or playing truant from Sunday School to catch tadpoles, like any other small boy. 'You were never particularly religious,' she said, at last.

'Mother, this has nothing to do with religion. No, that's wrong. It has, of course. But I am going out there to work, not preach. My profession gives me something to offer.'

'You could do just as much good here,'

28

she told him, quickly.

He shook his head. 'You have no idea of the difference. Here in Brambleden, a tiny village, you have two doctors. Luxurious security! In India you can travel for hundreds of miles without finding one qualified doctor.'

'Where exactly will you go?'

'To Calcutta first, and then I don't know. To remote villages, I expect, into the jungle, anywhere where I am most needed.'

'It will be dangerous.'

'Would you have me steer clear of danger?' he asked, reproachfully.

There was no reply to this, and within two months he had gone. Tirell declared ruefully that she had never realised how much work he did, but for Debbie there was an emptiness in her life which many people would not expect could be felt by mothers of fairly large families.

Bysshe of course was a comfort. He was a sociable, domesticated boy, ready to turn his hand to anything. In many practical ways he helped his mother in the school, and had a number of ingenious ideas, as when he made pencil suspenders for the pupils, attached to springs which fastened with brooches to their dresses, so that Debbie was no longer plagued by the constant cry of 'I can't find my pencil.'

He had shown no leaning towards any profession or trade, and Debbie had not pressed him. He seemed contented, and as the school prospered she came to depend more and more on him, for he combined the usefulness of a girl with the strength of a man. Playfully she called him her aide-de-camp.

It came therefore as an almost unendurable blow when, less than six months after Bertram had left them, Bysshe announced casually that he was going to sea.

At first Debbie did not understand. 'To sea? Where? How?'

'In a ship,' he replied, impatiently, 'not in a sieve.' He was irritated by what seemed to be her deliberate evasion, and also he was nervous, fearing her disapprobation.

She was at a loss. 'Where did you get such an idea?'

'Mother, I need a job.'

'You have one here.'

'That is for girls or boys, not for a man.'

'You feel I have done more for Bertram than for you,' she said; then, trying to be fair, went on, 'Well, if you have set your heart on it — I suppose I can afford it — It will mean a naval training college.'

'No, mother. That is not what I want. I intend to sign on as an ordinary seaman.'

'Seaman? You mean — you mean a deckhand?'

He smiled. 'Perhaps even a stoker, to begin with.'

'Oh, Bysshe! You cannot even consider such a thing. You don't understand what it would entail. You would have to mix with rough, violent characters, stand the most frightful hardships — '

Her words slid as smoothly from him as water from the proverbial duck's back. He was twenty-one. She could not prevent him. Either she must accept or alienate him for ever. She accepted, of course, and let him go, murmuring prayers for his safety, attempting to hide her qualms, and providing him with little comforts and luxuries which he suspected he would have to abandon before beginning his new life.

That was when Debbie grieved afresh for having given her youngest child into the care of Dolly and Christopher. How had she come to make such a mistake? For a mistake she now held it to be. Christopher had tempted her by promising to provide Ninian with a better life than she could offer, and at the time it seemed she had made a wise decision. Yet had she exercised more patience, waited until her school had become established, she could probably have afforded him as good an education as he was receiving from Christopher, if not one as fashionable and aristocratic.

It would not have been so bad had Christopher allowed her son to visit her, but this was forbidden, and the only time she saw him was in church on Sundays, when he and Benjy, scrubbed and in their Eton suits, sat decorously side by side in the Waldron pew.

She had to keep a watchful eye on her daughters and pupils, for Marlipins Academy must behave impeccably and set a good example, but often, as she knelt in prayer, she would raise her head and look across at that schoolboy and silently say, 'Ninian! Ninian!' as though with her thoughts to remind him, for she knew Christopher called him Thomas, and this she fiercely resented.

With her daughters she was strict and inclined to be demanding. It was not that she did not appreciate their assistance, but she had expended so much effort in making a success of the school that she expected equal zeal from them.

'Why don't we engage another servant?' Elianor demanded.

Debbie pursed her lips. 'Servants cost money.'

'We are doing well enough now.'

'Bertram's medical training was expensive.'

Elianor had nothing to say against this. It was taken for granted that money should be spent on preparing a son for a profession, whereas it could be wasted on a daughter. Daughters had a habit of cutting short their careers by marriage.

Yet Elianor persisted. 'Kitchen-maids are useless.'

It was true the last two had been summarily dismissed, one for theft, the other for drunkenness.

'I shall find a younger girl this time,' Debbie said, 'one I can discipline.'

The result was Violet, or, as she called herself, Vilet, with a strong accent on the vi. She came straight from an orphanage and was a scrawny little creature who looked chronically undernourished.

'A lot of use she will be!' Constance declared. 'She won't have the strength to lift the saucepans to the sink. Just our luck when Bysshe has taken a fancy to go to sea.'

Elianor felt sympathy for her brother. 'I don't blame him. Mother can't expect to keep all of us waiting on her hand and foot for ever.'

Constance sighed. 'We couldn't leave her just now. She's missing Bertram and Bysshe very much.'

'Well, I for one don't intend to be a prisoner for life.'

'Mother wants us to carry on the school after she has gone.'

'Gone!' Elianor exclaimed, with a sniff. 'She's only forty-two. She'll probably live another thirty years, and by that time we'll be wrinkled old maids, and you'll have grown a beard and I'll have a moustache.'

They laughed heartily over this distant and hardly credible prospect, and felt in a better mood.

Debbie did not propose to make her daughters life-prisoners, and certainly did not look so far ahead as her own demise, but she did care passionately for the school and resolved at all costs to uphold its success.

It seemed that year as if fate were on her side, for she had a new pupil, the first to be the daughter of titled parents. 'This is an honour for our school,' she assured Elianor and Constance and Faith. 'It will guarantee our prosperity, and we must do nothing to jeopardise it.'

'Can we raise our fees?' Elianor asked.

'Later, perhaps. Lady Verrall has already received our prospectus, so we cannot change anything at present.'

'Lady Verrall,' Faith murmured, impressed. 'I have never met a real lady.'

Debbie remembered, a little belatedly, that real worth did not lie in worldly glory. 'You have met many real ladies. They do not require to have titles.'

'Who is the girl's father?' Constance asked, practically.

'Sir Simon Verrall is in the diplomatic service.'

'What do we call the daughter?' Faith wanted to know.

'Her name is Lucy, and she will be treated exactly the same as the other pupils.'

'Exactly?'

'Well,' Debbie allowed, 'almost. Her mother has asked that she may have a room to herself.'

There was both pleasure and excitement in Debbie's voice, and the three girls felt their spirits rise. Their mother had not sounded so happy since Bertram and Bysshe had left them. Even Elianor, the discontented one, conceded that there was much to be said for running a really first-class school. It was like the dawn of a new era.

5

Worm or beetle — drought or tempest
— on a farmer's land may fall,
Each is loaded full o'ruin.

Will Carleton.

People declared they would never forget that
magnificent spring of 1893. The sun shone
and the dew fell, and all the budding and
the blooming was a month ahead of average.
It seemed as though nature wished to make
amends for the dreary and terrible winter
of 1890 and the backward spring of 1891
with its widespread outbreak of Russian
influenza.

At Marlipins Rose whistled as he worked,
and Alice hummed like a bee, and Joe-Ben
could not bear to drag himself away from
the woods and the meadows. All day he
roamed the countryside, drawing-book and
pencil in hand, making those notes and
sketches which later would form the true
and intimate pictures of wild life which
adorned his books.

'I wonder you bother to come in to sleep,'
his mother grumbled.

'I would not, but spring nights grow chilly towards morning. I've never known such a season, such energy. It's as if every leaf were straining to reach the light, to be born.'

A shadow crossed his face, and Alice knew what had caused it. He was thinking of those springs when Joan had been with him, sharing the joy, herself as wild as the creatures of the earth.

'Let's hope the summer will be as good,' she said, hoping to interrupt his thoughts, 'And then perhaps Rose can make a profit. No man likes a woman to earn more than he does.'

Joe-Ben laughed. 'With their Rational Dress and cricket and golf and tennis women will soon be beating men on all counts. Maybe they'll throw away their corsets and go out to work while we stay at home and feed the babies.'

'Don't be silly!' His mother exclaimed, a little crossly. 'It will never come to that. It's against nature.'

As far as the weather was concerned, nature appeared determined to make it a year of excesses, for that spring marked the beginning of one hundred and thirteen days of drought, the worst for fifty years. The early promise of the crops was not fulfilled, some failed entirely and the milk yield dropped as the grass became exhausted. Fortunately for the household of Marlipins there was a spring which rose in the hill, above the wood called Tiger's Heaven, and this did not run dry, as many of the wells did.

The pupils of the school had no farmers' problems. They rejoiced in the fine weather and persuaded Debbie to allow them to have many of their lessons out of doors. At first she was dubious.

'It will mean carrying chairs back and forth.'

'Oh, Mrs Aylwin, may we not sit on the grass?'

'The grass may be dry, but the ground is damp. You do not think so, because you can't see it. Have you never observed that the paving-stones look damp when the weather is hot and dry?'

'Oh, yes, ma'am,' replied a pupil who was a country girl. 'The people say 'the stones heave,' and there will be dry weather.'

'That means the air is raising the damp from the ground.'

'This year is different,' objected Lucy Verrall. 'In some places the earth has cracked widely enough for me to insert my hand.'

Debbie had not noticed this, but when she consulted Rose, he said it was true. 'Your precious pupils and their chills and fevers!'

he teased her. 'You and Dolly were never afraid of the damp. You tramped around all year in the wet and muck.'

'We were farm-girls. Still — '

She decided to permit the outdoor lessons, but insisted rugs should be laid on the ground.

The pupils were delighted and attributed their victory to Lucy. 'If you hadn't said that about the cracks in the ground — Could you really get your hand down?'

Lucy winked. 'Well, my little finger.'

That she was popular Debbie could see, and she tried to avoid any favouritism, urging her daughters to do the same.

'Just because her parents are influential people — '

'You go to the other extreme,' Elianor told her.

'Oh, I don't think so. I only try to be fair.'

Of this she was certain, especially when she attempted to curb one or two of Lucy's unfortunate habits.

'Lucy, the other day I saw you reading a most unsuitable book.'

'It was only a novel by Miss Yonge,' Lucy explained, innocently.

'Little girls of thirteen are certainly too young to read novels.' Debbie spoke severely.

'And another thing. What is this I hear about your reading in bed?'

'Who has been telling tales?' Lucy asked, angrily.

'Never mind. It is a bad habit and injurious to your eyesight. Just because our only spare bedroom is at the top of the house, it does not mean you are unobserved. If your mother had not expressed the wish for you to have a room to yourself, you would have occupied a dormitory with the other pupils. As it is, I or Miss Elianor or Miss Constance will come when you are in bed and remove the candle, until we have broken you of the habit.'

Debbie went away satisfied that she had handled the matter with discretion. She did not realise she had left behind a rebellious girl who was also a resourceful one. The only other occupant of the top floor was Violet. It would be a simple matter, Lucy was sure, to bribe Violet to supply her with a stock of candles and matches.

It was a relief when that summer Term drew towards its end. Though the drought had broken, the ground was still parched and needed a prolonged rainfall, and there was a feeling of exhaustion among both people and animals.

'We'll have a bad autumn and winter,' Rose prophesied, 'whatever the weather. Everyone will be buying in fodder, and the price will go up to the sky.'

Joe-Ben agreed with him. 'The birds will suffer. There will be few berries or seeds. Some of the bushes in the hedgerows are shrivelled beyond recovery.'

This dejection was common throughout the countryside, though at Farncombes it was not so pronounced. Christopher complained that his lawns were ruined, and that some of the flower-beds seemed to be growing bundles of straw, but he was not concerned about food. Whatever they wanted they could afford to buy, and farmers would supply him gladly enough if he offered to pay them a little more than others did.

Dolly was always glad when it was time to prepare for the school holidays. She missed the boys, and if she could have had her wish would not have sent them away at all, though she thought they looked perfectly sweet in those smart Eton jackets, and if anyone asked her where they went to school — But who ever did ask her? The village people knew everything that happened, and she saw scarcely anyone from the outside world. Christopher, being by profession a 'gentleman', did not need to go anywhere, and so made few friends. He hunted, but only occasionally, for he imagined the county

41

gentry looked down on him as an Australian and not a dyed-in-the-wool aristocrat. He went shooting by himself, and whenever he felt like company was more at home in the public bar of the Half Moon.

On the whole he was less lonely than Dolly, for he had not been brought up, as she had, in the family atmosphere of Marlipins, and in the company of a beloved twin sister. Dolly would walk through the large lofty rooms of Farncombes, rooms which, though furnished, seemed lifeless and empty, and she would wonder what she was doing there, and what on earth had possessed Christopher to build such a great monstrosity of a house. Was he trying to impress her and her family? Was it a strange kind of revenge for having failed to possess Marlipins?

Only when the boys were home did the house come to life, and as always Dolly's spirits lifted at the prospect of the long summer holidays. Boyish voices and laughter would echo through the empty rooms. Feet would run instead of walking. Servants would grumble about the mud to be cleaned from the floors. It would be living instead of stagnating.

Now that they were fourteen she reckoned Benjy and Tom would be real companions. She would arrange outings for them, take them further afield than they had been before. They could visit places in West Sussex, go by train to Chichester, the county town, or see the famous Arundel Castle. There was so much to do. It would be a holiday for her as well as for them.

Only one disappointment as usual clouded her pleasure. Christopher had expressly forbidden her to take the boys to Marlipins. 'You are not to go anywhere near the place.'

'That's what you say every time they come home.'

'And I mean it.'

'Well, I reckon Debbie has a right to see her son now and again.'

'She renounced that right when she entrusted him to me.'

'We never adopted him legally.'

'No matter. I have raised him and educated him.'

'I don't know why you were so anxious to do so.'

'Benjy needed a brother, and since you were unable to have any more children — '

'That's not true!' Dolly burst out. 'You know it was you — ' She stopped and turned and moved away. It was some time since Christopher had raised his hand against her, but she was still afraid of his anger. Though she was sure Benjy was not Christopher's son, she could not prove it. It seemed a long time ago, her brief and passionate affaire with Peter Baker, and she had heard no word from him since he left the district. Well, why should she? He had been a wanderer, a bird of passage.

All the same, she had never understood Christopher's fondness for Debbie's boy. He called both children his sons, yet his partiality for Tom was obvious. It was as if he were aware of some relationship between them of which Dolly was ignorant, and the fact that he denied any access by Debbie to her son pointed to his deep possessiveness.

Even while the boys were babies he had made Dolly swear she would not reveal Tom's parentage to him.

'I see no sense in that,' she had objected.

'It's my wish. That is enough.'

She shrugged her shoulders. 'Anyway, someone will tell him. All the village knows who he is.'

'My boys will not hob-nob with the villagers.'

'The servants then. Servants are full of gossip.'

To counter this he engaged staff from other districts, and, as far as Dolly knew, Tom believed himself a Waldron born.

The two boys arrived home filled with holiday zest and joyfully anticipating the weeks of freedom before them.

'No more Latin!' Benjy cried. 'No more beastly algebra! I shall tear up my exercise-books.'

'You'll get into trouble if you do,' Dolly warned him.

'Not until September. Nothing frightful can happen until September, and that's ages and ages away.'

Tom was more temperate in his desires. 'May I come shooting with you, Father?'

Christopher consented, smiling. His whole person seemed to exude pride and pleasure, and Dolly reflected gratefully that his personal barometer would probably remain at 'Set Fair' for the next few weeks.

6

Unknown Territory.

The problem of birthdays had been one
which caused Christopher a considerable
amount of thought. There was less than
three months difference between the ages of
Benjy and Tom. They would be brought up
to believe themselves brothers, but the time
must come when they would realise it was
impossible that they should have the same
mother.

Christopher settled this in what Dolly
looked upon as his usual high-handed
manner. 'I shall change the date of Tom's
birth. It would be ridiculous if he were not
a year younger than Benjy.'

Dolly was shocked. 'You can't change
birthdays. Do you imagine you are God?'

'Silly girl! I can do as I please.'

'Debbie has Tom's birth certificate.'

'She has the registration of a child
name Ninian Aylwin. Our boy is Thomas
Waldron.'

'What will happen when Tom grows up
and has to sign legal documents? It will be

as if he doesn't exist.'

'Time enough to worry about that later.'

'Debbie will never give up her right to him.'

Christopher shrugged his shoulders. 'Who knows?'

'Well, I don't understand why you make such a fuss of Tom. He's not your son or mine.'

'Keep your voice down!' Christopher commanded, harshly. 'Do you want to have the servants' tongues wagging?'

'I don't care, but Benjy is old enough to notice that Tom is your favourite. I don't want him to feel hurt. Anyway, I would have thought my son — '

'Oh, yes! The son of my wife and my farm bailiff. You are lucky I didn't disown him. You are lucky I didn't send both you and the brat packing. But for my generous nature — '

'Generous nature? You? You asked me to return to you because you wanted to pretend Benjy was your son. You still do pretend. Why, then, do you favour Tom? It's a mystery to me.'

This conversation, or others similar, had taken place many times. Dolly was jealous of Christopher's preference for Tom, and could see no reason for it. Tom was a nice enough little boy, she allowed, but in her opinion not to be compared with Benjy. Tom was gentle, reliable, honest, but somewhat stolid; Benjy was quick, volatile, highly-strung. For Debbie's sake Dolly was prepared to treat Tom with kindness and consideration, but only on Benjy could she bestow her natural maternal love.

The boys appeared to notice no difference in the affection they received. For so long had they boarded at school that home was merely a series of holidays, to be anticipated with joy because of the freedom and treats and relaxation of rules. Dolly and Christopher were adjuncts to this happy mode of existence. To them the boys protested, at the end of each vacation, that they detested going back and wished holidays would last for ever. But actually, like most restless young creatures, they welcomed the change, and were glad to be among their friends again, were even resigned to the concentration on lessons.

The one constant factor in their life was their relationship with one another. So close in age were they that they could not remember a time when they were not together, and could not even visualise a prospect of separation. In scripture and in literature there was emphasis on the love of brothers, and this they took to be the norm. Almost everything they did, they did together. Friends were pleasant, but friends scattered during the holidays, to other environments, other communities, but brothers shared all events and memories of events. Where could they find a closer companionship?

Dolly's fears of the evil of favouritism were unnecessary in this case. Jealousy and envy had no place in the world Benjy and Tom inhabited.

When Tom returned from his shooting outing with Christopher, Benjy wanted to know all about it.

'It was splendiferous!' Tom exclaimed, with more than his usual enthusiasm, then added, in consolation. 'You wouldn't have liked it.'

'Why not?'

'The guns make a big bang.'

Benjy accepted this. He was ashamed of his fear of loud noises, and kept it a secret from everyone but Tom. It was embarrassing on such occasions as the letting off of fireworks, but Tom was ingenious in making excuses for Benjy's absence. To Benjy it was fortunate that he was not invited to go shooting. If he did, and flinched at each explosion, as he was sure he would, Christopher would despise him, and for

Christopher he had a secret admiration he would not confess even to Tom. It was wrong to keep anything from Tom, he felt, but perhaps in this case it didn't matter. It was not the custom to discuss one's feelings for one's parents.

The room the boys shared was, in their opinion, the best in the house. It was at the top of one of the two towers, right under the battlements, as good as living in a castle, and often at school they entertained the other boys with descriptions, somewhat embroidered, of the glories of their habitation.

'It's so high,' Benjy said, 'that we have to look down on the eagles as they fly past.'

'Bet you don't have any eagles,' someone objected.

'Well, sparrow-hawks anyway,' Tom amended. His fantasies were never quite so fantastic as Benjy's.

True enough the turrets were high. Christopher had seen to that. He wanted Farncombes to rise above the trees, and look down on the countryside.

The boys' room had a broad view of the rolling Sussex Weald. In the far distance rose the South Downs, and nearer clustered the woods and coppices and shaws as proof that East Sussex was still the most thickly afforested part of England, and that the day of the tree was not over. Around and between these woods lay the cultivated fields, the leys and the old pastures which had not felt the plough within living memory.

Also from the top of Farncombes could be seen Marlipins. Compared with the new Gothic house, Marlipins had a low, sprawling appearance, as though, rather than having been built, it had grown from the earth. To the boys it was interesting because, despite being their nearest neighbour, it was unknown territory.

At a young age, with the natural curiosity of children, they had questioned Dolly. 'Who lives there?'

'My mother, my sister, my two brothers, my sister-in-law, four nieces and two nephews.' That was after the death of her father.

The boys' eyes widened in astonishment. Such a wealth of relatives, so near, and they did not know them! 'Don't you never see them?'

'Sometimes,' Dolly admitted.

'Why don't we visit them?'

Children's questions were often embarrassing, but this was the most difficult Dolly had encountered. She decided truth was the safest course. 'Marlipins was the home of the Waldrons long ago, before your father's grandfather went to Australia.'

This was even more exciting. 'Then it's our home.'

'No. Your father wanted it but my family would not leave. They want it too.'

The small boys found this confusing, a kind of internecine warfare. To Benjy especially it was troubling. 'Is Father angry with you?'

'No. Why should he be?'

'Because your mother and — and all the others won't let him have the house.'

'He doesn't want two houses,' Tom said, practically. 'This one's big enough.'

'Will you take us to Marlipins?' Benjy asked.

'No, dear. I'm sorry. I can't.'

'Why not?'

'Your father does not wish you to go.'

That was when the mystery of Marlipins was born. The boys discussed it long and often, and as they grew older the subject did not lose its fascination. Even now, looking out on the familiar landscape, their eyes turned towards Marlipins.

'I can't understand why Father won't allow us to go and see them,' Tom said.

'It's a feud,' Benjy told him. Put that way it sounded far more romantic than a mere family quarrel.

'Well, it's not our fault, and now we're almost grown up — '

52

'I think there's something else.' Benjy's imagination was beginning to work. 'There's some mystery. Maybe there's danger and Father knows and doesn't want us to get hurt or killed or something.'

'What kind of danger?'

Benjy's imagination reached a blank wall. 'Anyway, they probably don't want to see us.'

'Don't be silly! People always want to see their relations, even when they hate them. That's what they mean when they say blood is thicker than water.'

'Mine isn't. At least, it's no thicker than the water in the hammer pond.'

'That's stagnant. But don't you let Mother know we play around there.'

'Oh, Mother's just scared. Women usually are. Almost everything we really want to do is forbidden.'

'It's better than school anyhow.'

In the first flush of homecoming Benjy agreed with him whole-heartedly, and they went down to supper.

Grown-up conversation was rarely worth full attention, but during the meal Dolly happened to say, 'The boys have broken up early this year, haven't they?' And they pricked up their ears.

'Not particularly,' Christopher replied.

'Debbie's pupils don't go home for another three days.'

'Oh, she's a law unto herself.' There was no mistaking the contempt in Christopher's voice. Tom kicked Benjy's ankle.

It was a warm, windless night and at bedtime the boys went to the wide-opened window of their room.

'It smells like the jungle,' Benjy said, dreamily.

'You've never been to a jungle.'

'All the same I know how it smells.'

'That's because of the drought. Everything seeded too soon. We'll have early blackberries if they've not shrivelled.'

'Why did you kick me?' Benjy asked.

'Because of what Father said. Debbie is mother's sister. She has the school. You could hear he didn't like her, couldn't you?'

'Perhaps she did him a wrong.' Benjy was not aware that he was defending Christopher. His mind moved from head-mistress to pupils. 'Think of all those girls!'

'Think what about them?'

Benjy was not quite sure what he meant. He and Tom had recently moved from the period of despising girls, or pretending to despise them, to a stage when they suspected women might have some rather interesting uses. It was not yet easy to talk about, even

54

between themselves. Benjy stumbled into an explanation.

'Think of them all asleep over there.'

Tom thought, and was surprised that it should be such an exciting idea. 'I say,' he said, hastily, 'we'd better get to bed. They let us stay up late tonight.'

'They always do, the first night. Here, wait a minute! Look!'

Tom looked. 'What is it?'

'A light in one of the top rooms.'

'What of it?'

Benjy was struck by inspiration. 'Wouldn't it be fun if we went over there and looked.'

'Looked?'

'Through the window.'

'That's a dotty idea.'

'Why? Didn't we say we'd do some wild and dangerous things, these hols? You know how boring it gets sometimes.'

'You can't look through an upstairs window.'

'Yes you can, silly! There's only one storey above the ground floor at Marlipins. We could find a ladder or climb a pipe.'

As though the sound of the name had fired him, Tom agreed. There was no problem about getting out of the house, no need to creep. So spacious and solid was it that they simply had to walk along a corridor, down

55

a lesser staircase, and let themselves out of one of the back doors.

Marlipins was less than a mile away. They went across the grounds which had once been fields, through a small wood, past the hammer pond, and there they were on the farm land. It was a glorious night, no moon, but a sky massed with stars like frozen fireworks.

Their hearts beating fast with excitement they came first to the school wing of the house, though they did not know this was what it was, and there was the light shining above them.

Benjy clutched Tom's arm. 'Look there!'

It could not have been more convenient. From the wall projected a small outhouse with a flat roof. It was even provided with a window and a window-sill. For two active boys it was no obstacle at all.

As quietly as possible they clambered up and moved in. But one difficulty they had not foreseen. The window was too high above the outhouse roof, and though they stood on tiptoe their heads were twelve inches or more below the glass.

They had reached an impasse, and it looked as though they would have to turn round and go home. It was most disheartening.

Then Benjy had an idea. 'I'll climb on to

your back.' Tom was not sure, but Benjy urged him. 'I'm lighter than you are.'

Tom bent down and steadied himself against the wall, and Benjy mounted, first to his knees, and afterwards put his hands on the sill, drawing himself to his feet. They were both quiet for a few minutes, after which Tom whispered, 'Are you going to be all night?'

Slowly, reluctantly it seemed, Benjy let himself down. 'Well, what is it?' Tom asked.

'It's a girl. She's in bed.'

Tom breathed quickly. He felt a heat which was not of the night. The idea of 'girl' and 'bed' affected him strangely. This was something he had never seen. 'What's she doing?'

'Reading a book. She's very beautiful.'

Tom made up his mind. 'I must see her.'

'You can't.'

'Why shouldn't I? You did.'

'You're heavier. I couldn't hold you.'

'Yes, you could. When people stand on your back it doesn't matter whether they're eight stone or twelve stone.' This was pure invention, but Benjy allowed himself to be persuaded, because he knew it would be unfair to deny Tom the pleasure he had enjoyed.

Tom looked, and felt he could have watched for ever. It was a pity Benjy swayed and trembled, for it made it difficult to see properly. He moved one foot to try to spread his weight, and then several things happened at once. The back on which he was standing disappeared. He uttered an involuntary cry. The girl looked up, saw him and screamed. At the same time her arm which was holding the book shot out and knocked over the candle.

For a few seconds Tom clung to the window-sill with his fingers, but they were the longest few seconds he had known. He saw the girl's frightened face, saw her mouth open, her arm swing, the candle fall on to the bed, a flame shoot up.

He dropped to the outhouse roof. Benjy was already preparing to climb down. 'Come on!' he was urging. 'Hurry up!'

Tom followed him. 'We've got to warn them,' he shouted even before he reached the ground.

Benjy seemed not to hear him. 'Come on! We must run.'

Benjy wouldn't know. He hadn't seen. 'She knocked over the candle,' Tom explained. 'The room's on fire.'

'Oh, goodness! Let's get home quickly.'

'You don't understand. The room is on

fire, maybe the whole house.'

'Who would you tell?'

'The people here.'

In panic Benjy clutched him, as if to hold him back by physical force. 'You mustn't! They'd know we were here. They'd blame us.'

'That can't be helped.'

'What d'you think Father would do? He'd half kill us. It wasn't our fault, Tom. We must just keep quiet.'

'It was our fault. If she hadn't been startled — '

'There are lots of people in the house. The girl will tell them. She'll warn them before we could.'

'It *was* our fault. If we hadn't come — '

'All right. Maybe it was, but we can't do anything about it now, only get ourselves into trouble.'

Tom looked up. There was a glow behind the window. He felt sick with guilt, but perhaps Benjy was right. Benjy had disappeared into the darkness. Tom followed him.

7

But Madame Bad Luck soberly comes
    And stays — no fancy has she for
      flitting —
Snatches of true-love songs she hums,
    And sits by your bed, and brings her
      knitting.
      'Good and bad luck.' John Hay.

Lucy's scream awakened Violet. Usually the little kitchenmaid slept heavily, exhausted by hours too long and labour too strenuous, but that night was sultry, and her bedroom, designed for a boxroom, was too hot in summer and too cold in winter.

So she moved restlessly, only half asleep, and the scream roused her immediately. But for a few moments she hesitated to do anything. Perhaps Miss Lucy was having a nightmare. Better wait and listen. If she screamed again —

Life had taught Violet that minding her own business was the only way to avoid trouble. To be inconspicuous was next best to being invisible.

There was not another scream, but several

bumps, and sounds Violet could not identify. Reluctantly she got out of bed, went to the next room and knocked on the door. When there was no reply she went in, and could scarcely believe what she saw, Lucy had taken the large jug from her washhandstand, and was pouring water on the bed.

'Oh, Miss Lucy! Whatever are you doing?' Violet asked.

Lucy did not answer such a silly question. Smoke was rising from the hair mattress with an acrid smell which made her cough.

Violet took a step back. 'I'll go tell Mrs Aylwin.'

'You'll do nothing of the kind,' Lucy snapped. 'She'd be furious. You know she forbade me to — ' She thought she had put out the fire, but Violet's flinging open of the door had caused a draught, and the smouldering bedclothes burst into flame again. 'Oh dear! I've used all the water.'

She handed the jug to Violet and obediently Violet took it. She reckoned she was expected to go down to the kitchen, to the pump over the sink. But before either of them could move, the flames, as though released from bondage, had leapt up almost ceiling high and reached out to where Lucy's dressing-gown hung on the back of the door. The two girls

61

shrank back, first dismayed, then thoroughly frightened.

'We can't get through that door noways,' Violet said. Her voice quavered.

Lucy looked over her shoulder. 'Someone is outside.'

'Who?'

'I don't know. It was too dark to see properly, but there was a face.'

Violet went to the window, threw it open and leaned out. 'Nobody there.' She felt she ought to call, but did not know what to say. 'Hi!' she shouted, but as this sounded inadequate she added, 'Help!' wondering whether their predicament warranted such a dramatic cry.

Lucy had no doubts. Behind them was a roaring and a crackling as the flames ate up the wood, and the smoke made it almost impossible to breathe.

'We'll have to get out of the window,' Violet told her.

Lucy looked down. 'Oh, I couldn't! It's too high.'

'Can't be more than six foot to the roof.'

'I've no head for heights.'

'Well, if you was to put your hands on the sill and lower yourself 'twould be hardly any distance at all.'

'I tell you, I couldn't. In the gymnasium

I can't hang from the bars by my hands. I'm delicate.'

'We can't stay here.'

'Someone will come.'

'Yes, but will it be soon enough?'

The whole room was now alight. The heat was intense, and it could not be many minutes before the flames reached them.

'Listen!' Violet said. 'You climb on to the window-sill and I'll hold your hands and let you down slowly.'

'I'm too heavy for you. You'd drop me.'

'Course I wouldn't! I'm strong as a horse. Have to be, the work I do.'

A flame licked at the curtains. Lucy gave a cry and scrambled on to the sill. It would be quicker and safer to jump, but for her it was a psychological impossibility. She clutched Violet's hands and inched round so that she faced the wall. The rough bricks hurt her knees and her toes as she pressed inward, seeking a foothold.

For Violet it was as if her arms were being dragged from their sockets. She was leaning so far out that she thought she would lose her balance. 'Jump now!' she urged. 'It's no distance at all.'

She loosened her hold on Lucy's hands, but Lucy clung to her in a grasp she could not shake off. 'Let me go!' she implored.

Lucy was whimpering. 'My feet hurt. If I had some shoes — '

At that moment the window exploded in a spatter of broken glass and a tongue of flame came out and licked the wall of the house. Only then did Lucy let go, and collapsed on the roof of the outhouse. She did not know she had been holding the hands of a dead girl.

All night the occupants of Marlipins fought the fire. The parish fire-engine arrived with a fine galloping of horses, but it was only a token appearance, for the hose was not long enough to reach the hammer pond, which was the nearest water supply in any quantity. To make up for this the whole household, including the pupils, formed a human chain from the house to the hammer pond, passing continuous buckets of water hour after hour. As the news of the fire trickled through, Villagers came to relieve those who were exhausted. It was, as the local paper reported later, a magnificent effort, and although no part of the school wing could be saved they managed to preserve the rest of Marlipins from all but superficial damage.

By the following morning the weather had changed, and was windy and cloudy, with frequent heavy storms.

Joe-Ben found Debbie standing in the

rain, gazing at the wreck of what had been Marlipins Academy for Young Ladies.

He lifted his face to the sky. 'This is something for which we have to thank heaven. Had there been wind without rain, we might have had a secondary fire. Smouldering ruins are always a danger, but I don't think we need worry about Marlipins now.'

'Marlipins!' Debbie exclaimed, bitterly. 'Isn't this Marlipins?'

'Yes, a part of it. But we never used it much, did we?'

'It's my living, my home.'

'You'll have the insurance money. We can rebuild.'

'That's all very well. What happens to my pupils in the meantime? Will they wait without education while those long-winded builders pile brick upon brick? The repairs will take months.'

'Well, we can discuss those details later.' He paused, then went on, 'We are all terribly upset about poor little Violet. If only that had not happened.'

'It's a blessing it was not one of the pupils,' Debbie said, crisply.

Joe-Ben looked at her, shocked. 'Debbie! How can you say such a thing?'

'It's true, isn't it? She was an orphan. There's no one to make a fuss. Now if it had been a pupil, there would have been a lot of trouble. If it had been Lucy Verrall — well, I shudder to think what would have happened. It would have ruined me.'

'Violet died saving Lucy.'

'There you are, then!'

'What do you mean by that?'

'I mean Lady Verrall can scarcely blame us, considering I sacrificed one of my staff to save her daughter.'

'*You* sacrificed?'

'Certainly. I employed her, and I no longer have her. What would you call that but a sacrifice?'

'Debbie, I never thought — ' Joe-Ben said slowly, 'I never thought the day would come when I would be ashamed to have you as my sister. You've changed. You were a different woman when you were Ninian's wife.'

'Necessity made me what I am. When a young woman is left a widow with five children — '

'Six.'

Debbie was silent.

'Six,' Joe-Ben repeated. 'I think the iron entered your soul when you gave young Ninian to Christopher.'

'Not iron,' Debbie corrected him. 'More likely a splinter of ice in my heart. All right,' she agreed, wearily, 'maybe I ought to hate myself, but I don't. I educated my children, made Bertram a doctor — '

'I'm not denying your success.'

'Well,' she smoothed back her hair, 'I can't stay here talking. There's so much to be done. I have to arrange for all the children to go home. They can't leave today, of course. The poor creatures are exhausted after being up all night and lifting those heavy buckets. Mother is making up beds on the floor of the parlour. As for me and the three girls, I think we should use Tirell's surgery, don't you?'

Joe-Ben laughed. 'I'm not getting involved in any domestic disputes. You must settle that with Tirell.'

'I will. It will only be a temporary disturbance. I have sent telegrams to all the parents. They can either fetch their daughters or I will put them on the train tomorrow.'

The first parent to arrive was Lady Verrall. She came like an avenging angel to Battle Station, and thence by the rather rickety station cab.

'She came to battle in more ways than one,' Joe-Ben said. 'There should have been trumpets all along the route.'

'Where is my poor child?' Lady Verrall demanded. 'Is she still alive, or are you deceiving me?'

'She is perfectly well,' Debbie assured her.

'Well? What are these dreadful cuts on her face?'

'Just one or two scratches from broken glass.'

'Scratches? They have spoilt her beauty. Now she will never find a husband.'

'Nonsense!' Debbie started to say, but bit her lip. 'They will soon heal.'

'I hurt my feet,' Lucy told her mother.

'How did you do that?'

'Getting out of the window.'

Lady Verrall sucked in her breath. 'Merciful God! Was that the only exit? Do you mean to tell me, Mrs Aylwin, that you do not provide fire-escapes?'

Debbie began to lose patience. 'Had there been fire-escapes you would have seen them. But there was no necessity. This house is lowly built, and there was no more than six feet between Lucy and safety. Unfortunately she is of a nervous disposition. However, she was in no danger.'

Lucy smiled ingratiatingly. 'That's right. I hung on to Violet, and she was burnt to death.'

Debbie could have strangled the child, but at that moment her attention was fully occupied with Lady Verrall who, on hearing

68

such news from Lucy, promptly fainted dead away.

It was a relief to see Lady Verrall and her daughter depart, although Lady Verrall's last remarks were by no means reassuring.

'You mean to say that Lucy has lost everything, all her beautiful clothes? And the other children are in the same predicament? Well, I can promise you one thing, Mrs Aylwin. You certainly have not heard the last of this.'

8

The deep damp hole where the nettles grow.

It was a distinction Violet could never have expected, to be the central figure of an inquest and, what was more, to have her name in a Sussex newspaper. There was not a picture available, for no one had ever thought to photograph her, but she was described as a 'brave girl' who had performed a 'courageous act'.

Lucy, to her credit, made no attempt to underestimate Violet's deed. 'I'd have died if she hadn't come. The door was on fire, so there was no way to escape except by the window. Yes, there was a roof below, but it was too high for me. I'm no good at jumping.'

Her mother was not over-sympathetic. 'I really fail to discover in what areas you do shine. To knock over the candle was pure clumsiness.'

'I couldn't help it,' Lucy said, sulkily. 'I was frightened. I saw a face at the window.'

Had her mother not been well bred she

70

would have sniffed at this. 'You imagined it, I expect.'

'I did not. It was horrible.'

'How could you know? It was dark outside. The trouble with you, miss, is that you read too many novels. At your next school, you shall share a dormitory with the other girls, then perhaps you will be safe.'

'My next school? Shall I not go back to Marlipins?'

'Certainly not! It is far from being a suitable establishment. I wish I had not sent you there in the first place. The whole business has made me the laughing-stock of my friends. All that unfortunate publicity!'

The publicity, however, was short-lived, for there was nothing scandalous or mysterious about the event, though one reporter did use the word 'scandalous' when stating that the school was not provided with a fire-escape.

Violet was buried quietly in an obscure corner of the churchyard, Joe-Ben and Rose being the only mourners. Easily the two of them carried the coffin, so small and light it was.

The vicar had approached Debbie regarding the grave and she had made her position quite clear to him. 'I employed the girl as kitchen-maid, but she was with us scarcely more than a year. As far as I know, she was

71

without relatives. No, we shall not erect a stone. You could not expect us to do so. Bury her where you think fit, Vicar. After all, the whole churchyard is consecrated ground, isn't it?'

There were no flowers on Violet's grave, but a few days after the funeral there was one visitor, young Thomas Waldron. He tried to persuade Benjy to accompany him, but Benjy was definite in his refusal.

'What d'you want to see a grave for? It's morbid, looking at graves. Churchyards are morbid anyway.'

'I just want to see where she's buried.'

'Why?'

It was difficult to explain. 'Well, it was our fault, wasn't it? Sort of.'

'No, it wasn't. It was that stupid girl knocking over the candle.'

'We shouldn't have run away.'

Benjy did not agree, but he knew how tiresome Tom's conscience could be. He'd had trouble with it before.

'It wouldn't have made any difference. By the time we got down off that roof the room was blazing. If we'd woken up the people in the other part of the house, it would have been too late.'

Tom could follow Benjy's logic, but in no way did it assuage his sense of guilt. 'We should have stayed and helped the girl out of the window.'

'There wasn't much of a fire then. She was pouring water on it. Besides, she wouldn't have come. It was your face that scared her, and no wonder.'

Tom made a lunge at him. Benjy ducked, and hoped he had diverted Tom from his unhealthy outlook.

All the same Tom went to Brambleden church and asked the sexton to direct him to the grave of the girl who had died in the Marlipins fire.

The sexton was not encouraging. 'We don't want a crowd of sightseers coming around.'

'I only want to look at it.'

'That's what they'd all want, look and stare as if it was a raree-show. Graves is graves, and that's all there is to 'em.'

'I'd only stay a minute or two.'

Reluctantly the sexton gave way. 'You're a rum youngster. Well, if you want it you'll find it at the bottom. Over there, far as you can go, next to the hedge.'

Carefully Tom picked his way across the churchyard, between the graves, trying not to step on them, for when he was very young he had been told that to walk on graves was a heinous offence, almost as bad as taking the

Lord's name in vain, but certainly clearer to understand.

From the point where the gravestones ended he felt free to run down the slope. Here the grass was disturbed in only one or two spots. It was awaiting its future inhabitants.

The solitary grave at the bottom could not be mistaken. It stood out, bare and bleak, not one blade of grass softening its covering of Sussex clay. In a few months, Tom knew, it would be just a green mound, only to be distinguished by its gentle swell, and later perhaps not even by that. He did not know which condition was more sad, its present rawness or the future when there would be nothing to remind anyone that the little kitchen-maid had ever lived.

He walked home in a subdued state of mind and as he passed Marlipins he averted his face. Never, he decided, did he want to go near the farm again. It made him feel ashamed and that was one of the most unpleasant feelings he had experienced.

At Marlipins they were more or less settling down. The boarders had all gone home, which relieved the congestion of the house, and Debbie and her three daughters had been allocated two bedrooms between them. Insurance officials had appeared, to make assessments, and then disappeared, apparently to perform some higher arithmetic. When this was done there would no doubt be compensation forthcoming, and then builders to be employed.

Debbie was assured by the family that all would be plain sailing, but as August drew to its end she had received blow upon blow.

'Every one,' she said, tearfully, 'every single one, without exception.' She flourished a fan of envelopes. 'All the parents have written to say they are taking their daughters away from me.'

'They may fear the rebuilding will take too long,' Alice suggested.

'I've promised them it won't. I have sworn we shall reopen before Christmas, and I am determined we shall. Even if we have to commandeer your parlour, mother, I'm sure you won't mind.'

Rose shuddered. 'Were you thinking of turning a cow-house into a dormitory?'

'I am serious,' Debbie said, angrily. 'I will do anything — '

'Are you proposing to install a fire-escape?' Joe-Ben asked, with some concern.

'Yes, I am, and this I have told the parents. But what is the use? That monstrous Lady Verrall is set on ruining me. It is all her doing.'

'Are you accusing her of influencing the parents?' There was a twinkle in Rose's eye.

'Why not? They are snobs. They would take notice of her.'

'Never mind, dear!' Alice spoke soothingly. 'You will soon find other people.'

'What makes you think so? A bad name travels far, and a bad reputation sticks like glue. I don't know what I shall do.'

'You still have me,' Daisy said.

Debbie looked at her pityingly. It was strange how slight was the attention Daisy commanded. There was nothing wrong with her, but surely Joe-Ben's daughter should have a more outstanding personality. 'Yes, I still have you,' Debbie agreed, 'but while the house is being restored you will have to attend the village school.'

Daisy grimaced. 'I'm nearly too old. They are all babies.'

Debbie nodded. 'You'd have to leave soon anyway. Well, you must see what your father says about it.'

Joe-Ben moved uneasily. Debbie's practical outlook and worldly wisdom jarred on him, and he sensed implied criticism in her reference to his paternal responsibility. He realised he was by no means a perfect father, but he thought he would have done better had not the family from the very first attempted to force him to put the baby in Joan's place. Against this he rebelled strongly. The child had cost Joan her life. He could not forget this, try as he might. So, without being openly neglectful, he had been content to allow his mother to raise the child, and now, with Daisy almost a woman, she was no closer to him than were Debbie's children.

Alice came nearer to understanding Daisy, who most needed her and who, being Joe-Ben's daughter, was especially dear to her. From an early age the child was shown the pictures in Joe-Ben's books, and listened while her grandmother read to her Joe-Ben's stories of the birds and animals living their private lives on man's doorstep and yet inhabiting a different world.

It was a joy to Alice to talk of Joe-Ben. 'Your father is famous,' she said.

Daisy had few comparisons. 'As famous as the Queen?'

'Well, famous in a different way. He writes clever books which have beautiful pictures.'

'And what does the Queen do?'

'She rules us.'

'Who does Dada rule?'

Alice smiled. 'No one. Your dada is the best and kindest of men. You'll never meet a finer man than your dada.'

This affirmation Daisy accepted and absorbed inevitably, for Grandmother was the one person who bothered about her, and therefore Grandmother would never lie to her. She would have worshipped her father, had she been given the chance, but Joe-Ben did not look deeply enough into the little girl's eyes to see the love in them. Unintentionally but perceptibly he repulsed her, and Daisy, who could not swerve from her belief in his excellence, concluded she herself must be at fault. Obviously she was not worthy of such a father. So she grew into a lonely, unsociable girl. She made no intimate friends among the pupils, who were inclined to mistrust her. Was it not like an enemy in the camp, to have the headmistress's niece among them?

Each day, when school work was over, Daisy returned to the family part of the house, to be submerged in a crowd of grown-ups. Even Faith, her youngest cousin, was three years older. There was no one in whom she could confide. She would have liked to remain at school, share a dormitory with the boarders. Perhaps then she might have joined in their pursuits, learnt their secrets, and they would not have whispered and laughed in front of her. But she was afraid to suggest such a thing to Aunt Debbie. Aunt Debbie, she knew, thought her a fool, and why not, since she was usually at the bottom of the class?

And Joe-Ben, so gentle that he would not have tweaked the whiskers of a field-mouse, was blind to the suffering of his child.

9

There's a daisy; I would give you some
violets, but they withered.

Shakespeare.

'It's all very well,' Rose said. 'I sympathise
with Debbie about the fire, though if she
had used some common sense it could have
been avoided. Trusting that child alone in a
bedroom with a candle!'

'Easy to have hindsight,' Joe-Ben reminded
him.

'Yes. Well, what's done can't be undone.
But now I have Debbie and her three girls
on my hands, and not a penny piece between
them, so far as I can see. She should have
accumulated a nest-egg, the fees she charged
for that school, but she seems to have
spent it all. What with Bertram's medical
training, and sending money to Bysshe, who
apparently jumped ship and is now a kind of
beachcomber — '

'Debbie hasn't had an easy time since
Ninian died.'

'No, and what farmer ever has an easy
time? People imagine farmers reap a continual

80

harvest and can feed regiments. It reminds me of when we had all the relations of Father's fancy-woman foisted on us.'

'Let's forget Frankie and Sarah. That's in the past.'

'Debbie and her family are not.'

'They'll rebuild before long. But you used to grumble about the school.'

'I know. Some of the kids were a nuisance, hanging around the farm. Still, Debbie couldn't have chosen a worse time to have a fire. I don't know how I'll get through the winter.'

It was not the first time Rose had expressed such a fear. Farmers, by their dependence on the vagaries of the weather, were prone to prophesy disaster, but Joe-Ben had to allow that the early spring, followed by the long drought, was liable to cause difficulties, and if it should prove to be a bad winter —

'Root crops will help,' he pointed out. 'There's time for the swedes to grow to good size.'

'Yes, and they'll taste in the butter. Even taint the milk if I give too many. The hay-ricks are half their usual size.'

'You'll have to buy fodder towards spring.'

'What! Pay six pounds a ton for old hay?'

'You reckon that's what it will be?'

'I do. No, I'll have to cull the herd.'

'That's a pity.'

'Can't be helped. There's some old strappers I can spare for the butcher. I dursn't dare deprive the in-calf heifers, and I've a fair number of those. What I can't stomach is to look across at Farncombes and see those acres Christopher has wasted on grass he keeps cut to the bone, and Japanese flower-trees, and yews his men are mutilating, trying to make peacocks and suchlike of 'em.'

'He's kept some fields,' Joe-Ben reminded him.

'Yes, but for what? I could do with renting them, only I know Christopher would surely refuse, for spite.'

'Do you think he still wants Marlipins?'

'He'd give his right arm for it. That monstrosity of a house he's built is only a salve for his disappointment.'

Suddenly Joe-Ben made up his mind. 'Listen! I've been thinking. I can spare some cash, to tide you over. Not a great deal, because there's something else I have to do.'

Rose had the grace to feel ashamed. 'I shouldn't be belly-aching. You've done enough. You paid for the new barn.'

'If five hundred would help — '

'It would be a godsend,' Rose replied, frankly. 'I'd ask Tirell, but — well, paying off the mortgage took most of the money her father left her, and people seem to think doctors' bills can be settled last of all.'

'Tirell is a brick.'

'I know. I don't deserve her.'

'Why do you say that?'

'Well, a small farmer isn't much of a catch. I work from daylight to dark, and she's on call twenty-four hours of the day. We don't see a lot of each other. You're the one she should have married.'

'Nonsense!' Joe-Ben exclaimed, hastily. 'If Joan hadn't come along, I don't suppose I should have found anyone. I'm not really the marrying kind.'

To himself he added. 'Nor the fathering kind I don't suppose.' He was experiencing a few stabs of conscience concerning Daisy. Since the fire he had often come upon her wandering around aimlessly, and the sight irritated him. Considering the dilatory methods of the insurance company it looked as though the school wing would not be rebuilt for several months at least, and he thought that Debbie or one of her girls should have given Daisy private tuition.

He broached the matter to Debbie and was given a poor reception. 'That is too much to expect,' she said, flatly. 'We can't waste our time on one child.'

He was annoyed. 'I would pay for the lessons. In any case, I don't see that you and the girls have much to occupy you at present.'

'Men never understand how much women have to do.'

'I've not seen you helping Mother in the dairy or the poultry yard.'

'I am no longer a farm girl,' Debbie said, coldly, 'and Elianor and Constance and Faith have not been brought up to that kind of life. Let Daisy learn something of farming. She's unlikely to be suitable for any other career.'

Joe-Ben left her before they should quarrel openly. He rarely lost his temper, but now Debbie's attitude angered him. How dared she infer that Daisy was practically a moron? How dared she, country-born and -bred, relegate farming to the realm of the unskilled and the unqualified? Daisy was his daughter and Joan's. Was she really so stupid?

It did not occur to him that Daisy was deserving of sympathy and compassion. It was his pride which was hurt, his pride which demanded that the girl should be given a chance.

Before his resentment should cool he took

a trip to London to seek advice from such experts as his publisher, his agent and his solicitor, and when he returned he was satisfied wheels had been set in motion to do what was manifestly his duty.

Three weeks later he announced the result, and it was to Debbie he first spoke. After all, she it was who had caused him to take such steps.

'I have made arrangements for Daisy to go away,' he said.

Debbie nodded approval. 'An excellent idea. It is rarely satisfactory for a child to be taught by relatives. There cannot be the same discipline. Where will she be going?'

'To a finishing school in Switzerland.'

Debbie's astonished eyes were as round as buttons. 'Finishing school? Switzerland?'

'Yes. It is run by a Madame de Valmore. She has the highest references, and I'm told that she has finished the daughters of half the aristocracy of Europe. That, of course, is an exaggeration.' Joe-Ben smiled. 'Tell me, how does one finish a young girl?'

'I never heard such nonsense in all my life.'

'You said it was an excellent idea.'

'To send her away, yes. But a finishing school! It will cost a fortune.'

'I think I can manage it. I have a new

book coming out in the spring.'

'A sheer waste of money. A child like Daisy!'

'What is the matter with Daisy?'

'Nothing specific, but — Well, I mean — ' For a few moments words failed Debbie, so furious was she. 'If she had talent — ' eventually she continued, 'talent like yours. Or some other kind. But she is always bottom of the class. She is not very bright.'

'Isn't that a reason for having her taught to be charming? I understand that is one of the aims of a finishing school.'

'If you have money to throw away,' Debbie said, bitterly, 'you might throw it in a direction where it is most needed. Remember, I have three daughters to support.'

'I'm sure they could find work,' Joe-Ben told her, bluntly. 'Their teaching experience — '

'I need them to help me with the school.'

'The school is not yet rebuilt, and you have no pupils.'

'Sometimes, Joe-Ben, you can be very nasty.'

'Well, let us not quarrel. I want to ask you a favour. Will you break the news to Daisy?'

'Why don't you tell her?'

Joe-Ben wriggled uncomfortably. It reminded

Debbie of the days when he had been a little boy and his grandfather had tried to force him to kill some animal. 'I don't like to see women cry,' he replied, lamely.

Debbie laughed. 'Oh, Daisy won't shed any tears. She'll probably be glad to go. She has no friends here.'

Believing this to be true, Debbie made no effort to be tactful when telling Daisy of the plans made for her.

'Your father is sending you away to school.' She waited for some response from the girl, but Daisy neither moved nor spoke. 'The school is in Basle, Switzerland, and it is extremely expensive. You should be grateful for such an opportunity.'

Daisy spoke then. 'So he is getting rid of me at last.'

'What do you mean, getting rid of you?'

'He's always hated me.'

'What rubbish you talk, girl! He is your father. How can he hate you? Do you suppose I could hate my children?'

'You didn't die when they were born.'

'Really, Daisy, there are times when you sound like an idiot. You should be rejoicing at your good fortune. The autumn term begins in three weeks' time, and before that you have to go to London to be fitted out with a new wardrobe. When you come home for Christmas you will be quite the young lady.' Debbie paused, and added, cryptically, 'I hope.'

Daisy said no more. In fact, she did not express to anyone her feelings about her future. She was taken to London and furnished with clothes of such smartness and elegance as she had never before worn.

Debbie's girls were too well brought up to display envy, but Faith could not help asking, 'Aren't you enraptured? It must be blissful to have so many gorgeous new dresses.'

Daisy shrugged her shoulders. 'It's all right. But they don't make me any different. I feel the same.'

'She must be made of stone,' Faith declared.

But one morning, a few days before she was due to leave for Switzerland, when her luggage was already packed, Daisy was missing. For several hours no one thought anything of it; Daisy often went for long walks alone. When teatime had come and gone, however, there was concern which changed to alarm as her pony came home, saddled and bridled.

'Why didn't someone tell me?' Joe-Ben demanded.

It had not seemed important, they informed him.

'Well, why didn't you notice her pony had gone?'

It had not occurred to them to look, he was told. In guilt and anger he immediately formed a search-party, on foot and on horseback, and they set out to scour the countryside.

Darkness had fallen when they found Daisy, in a wood some six miles away. She was sitting on the ground, cold, hungry and with a broken ankle.

They got her home, and Tirell treated her and put her to bed. 'Don't bother her with questions until tomorrow,' Tirell told Joe-Ben. 'She needs a good night's rest.'

But for Joe-Ben there was no sleep. He was racked with remorse. All these fourteen years since Joan's death, he thought, he had neglected the child. How could he have been so selfish, so callous? Was it not a slight on Joan, that he had cared so little for her child? What would he have felt if she had been killed or seriously injured? He would never have forgiven himself. Well, he would make amends now. Thank God it was not too late!

He was up early in the morning, sufficiently humbled to ask Tirell if he might see his daughter, and when he was given permission he ran up the stairs, his heart brimming with relief and gratitude.

So searching had been his emotions of the night that he was not sure what to expect — perhaps tears and outstretched arms, perhaps a white, pain-racked face.

At sight of the real Daisy he was suddenly shy. She looked so calm, sitting up in bed, and she did not smile as he entered the room.

'Hullo!' she greeted him.

'How do you feel, my dear?' He had wanted to say 'my darling,' but that was an expression he had never used to her.

'All right,' she replied. 'My foot hurts, though.'

'I expect it does.'

'I wouldn't have fallen off,' she assured him, quickly, 'but I hit my head on a branch.'

'It was foolish to ride so far by yourself, and without telling anyone you were going.'

'Oh, I wasn't just riding. I was running away.'

Remorse flooded him afresh. 'My poor dear child! Why didn't you tell me? Do you look upon me as an ogre? I wouldn't have made you go to school. Not for the world would I have forced you, if I had realised you dreaded it so much.'

Half expecting her to throw herself into his

arms he was stricken with surprise when she stared coldly at him.

'Dreaded it? Don't be silly! I was looking forward to it.'

'Then why did you — '

'I was trying to save you money. Aunt Debbie said it was an extremely expensive school, and when I saw how much the clothes cost — well, I mean I thought it would be cheaper to get rid of me if I ran away.'

He was shocked. 'Did you imagine that was why I was sending you to school?'

'Well, wasn't it?'

'Heavens, no! Of course not! It was because of the fire, and because you deserve a better education than Aunt Debbie was giving you. I was doing it entirely for your own good.'

Her expression was sadly cynical for her age. 'That's what they always say. Still, if you really can afford it — '

Try as he might, he could not retain that feeling of warmth and affection with which he had run up the stairs. Instead there was the irritation she so often roused in him. 'Of course I can afford it. Do you ever hear me complain about money?'

'Very well, then. I might as well go to Switzerland.' And she added practically, 'I'll miss a few weeks, till my ankle heals, so perhaps you'll get a reduction in fees.'

91

10

For truth itself has not the privilege
to be spoken at all times and in all sorts.
Michel de Montaigne.

For Tom it was a relief to be back at school,
to forget, or to try to forget, the Marlipins
fire. The routine of lessons and sport had
a soothing effect and responsibilities were
slight. So long as he kept to the rules, Tom
knew, he would not get into trouble. There
was no fear that by foolishness he might
cause the death of a human being.

As the Christmas holidays approached he
found himself once again brooding over what
he had done, and almost dreading the return
home.

'You know, it was our fault,' he said to
Benjy.

Benjy was bored with the whole subject
of fires and Marlipins, and considered it an
obsession of which Tom should be cured.
'All right. If you want to believe you're to
blame, you can. But don't count me in.'

'What do you mean? We were together.'

'Yes, but if you hadn't climbed on my

back, though you knew you were too heavy for me, the girl wouldn't have seen your face at the window, and she wouldn't have had a shock and knocked over the candle, and — '

'Oh, shut up!' Tom was silent for a few minutes, and then he said, 'I suppose we ought to own up.'

'Who should we tell?'

'I don't know. Somebody. Anybody. Father, perhaps.'

'And what good would that do? The girl would be just as dead.'

Tom thought about it and decided that Benjy was right. It was a pity, though, because he had been told that confession was good for the soul, and now he was left with a weight on his soul, like the heavy feeling in his belly when he had eaten too much pudding.

So they went back to Farncombes, and there were Christmas treats, and lots of scrumptious Christmas food, and both boys would have agreed that they were having a capital time.

Yet Tom had a nagging itch to go over to Marlipins, despite his resolve never to do so. From his bedroom window he could see that the rebuilding of the school wing was not complete; there was something black where the red tiled roof should be. He quashed the feeling until, towards the end of the vacation, he could bear it no longer.

He took the air-gun Christopher had given him for a Christmas present and said to Benjy, 'If Father or Mother want to know where I am, tell them I've gone shooting.'

'I'll come with you,' Benjy offered.

'No, I want to go alone.'

Benjy was disappointed. It was not like Tom to refuse his company. Only grown-ups, in his opinion, had these strange hankerings after solitude. He hoped it was not a sign that Tom was growing up. Benjy did not want to grow up if it meant that he and Tom must be separated.

Tom, unaware of Benjy's feelings, set out and, after taking a few pot-shots at rabbits, and missing them, came out in front of Marlipins. There were no men working on the wing that day, an occurrence all too common during the winter months, and one which annoyed Debbie exceedingly. She accepted with a pinch of salt the builders' explanation that such work could not be carried out during conditions of rain and frost, but the day of Tom's visit to the farm was a fine one.

'Excuses,' Debbie said to her mother, 'they always make excuses,' and she put on her coat and went to look at the wing, as she did most mornings.

It gave her a shock, and almost a pang of fear, to see her son standing there. She made a move to turn and go back, but by then he had seen her.

'I hope I am not trespassing,' Tom said, gravely.

'Well, that depends on your reason for being here.'

'I am Tom Waldron, from Farncombes. Who are you?'

'Mrs Aylwin, the headmistress of this school.'

'Oh! It was a terrible fire, wasn't it?'

'Terrible,' she agreed.

'It's taking a long time to build again.'

She sighed. 'It should be finished soon. There's only the roof to be done. That is tarpaulin to keep out the rain.'

As they talked she was studying him closely, with a kind of urgent hunger. He was a fine, strong boy, big for his age. She thought she saw a resemblance to Ninian. Was it his eyes, or was it in the firm set of his mouth and chin?

He felt the intensity of her scrutiny and it made him uneasy. 'I think I should be getting home.'

'No! No, don't go yet. That's a good gun you have.'

'Yes. It was a present from Father.'

The pride in his voice sent a wave of anger through her. Was it the gun he treasured, or the fact that Christopher had given it to him? Suddenly she was tempted to tell him the truth. What would he say if she told him, 'Christopher is not your father, nor is Dolly your mother'? What if she said, 'I am your mother'? There was nothing to prevent her. Sooner or later he would have to know who he was.

Love for the boy welled up in her. She thought, fiercely, I cannot control my natural maternal instinct, and to gain time she asked, 'Do you like going to Eton College?'

'Oh, yes! Father says it's the best. He always likes to give us the best of everything.'

She shivered. It was a cold, bleak day. Anger and temptation died away, and depression took their place. How could she have contemplated startling the boy with so abrupt a disclosure of his parentage? And if she did, what would Christopher tell him? From her knowledge of Christopher she suspected he would insist on his paternity, despite the harm it would do to Dolly and her already precarious marriage. Unscrupulous as he was, he would probably deny rape, and insist that Debbie had accepted him as her lover. No, Debbie decided, she was not ready to stir up all that mud, not even for the doubtful pleasure of saying, 'You are my son.'

Almost as though he had read her thoughts, Tom told her, 'You are awfully like my mother. I mean, to look at.'

Debbie smiled. 'I ought to be. We are twin sisters.'

'Then why don't you come and see her? You never visit each other, do you?'

'Well, not often. You see, there was a — a kind of family disagreement.'

'What kind?'

'You'll learn about it when you are older.'

'Why not now? I am fourteen, going on fifteen.'

'It was nothing to do with us,' Debbie said, firmly. 'Our mother was an Elphick before she was married, and Elphicks don't fall out. I still love Dolly as much as ever. Will you tell her that?'

Tom looked serious. 'I don't think I should. I don't think I should mention it. Father has forbidden us to come here.'

'He would!' The words were out before she could stop them.

Tom glanced at her disapprovingly. 'He must have had a good reason for doing so. Father always does what's right. I really must go now. Goodbye, Mrs Aylwin.'

He was gone. Debbie stood there, desolate, staring at the unfinished building, and at that moment it seemed to her that the school wing and the school itself were of little worth and importance.

Part Two

Part Two

1

Oh! the fluttering and pattering of the
  green things growing!
Talking each to each when no man's
  knowing:
In the wonderful white of the weird
  moonlight,
Or the grey dreamy dawn when the cocks
  are crowing.

Mrs Craik.

Respect, and even reverence, might be
accorded Joe-Ben by those who read his
books, but to his family he was becoming
the gentle eccentric, to be humoured and
smiled upon. Even Alice was somewhat
put out when one day a knock on the
door disclosed a group of half-a-dozen
tourists.

'The cheek of it!' she exclaimed later, to
Debbie. 'I was thinking they wanted to use
the jakes, but they asked could they see
Benjamin Joseph Elphick's study. 'Study?'
I says to them. 'What would Joe-Ben want
with a study?' Then one of 'em suddenly
blurts out, 'That's his mother!' And then

101

they stares at me like they was reading a finger post.'

'Joe-Ben is quite famous,' Debbie reminded her.

'Of course he is! But that's no call for me to let foreigners into my house.'

'Foreigners, were they?'

'Yes. From their talk they must have come from Kent, or even London.'

To his nieces Joe-Ben seemed old and slightly mad.

'He talks to the trees,' Faith remarked, in disgust.

Constance nodded. 'Maybe all nature writers are a bit peculiar. He flies into a frightful passion about the birds.'

Faith looked sceptical. 'I never saw Uncle Joe-Ben fly into a passion.'

'He doesn't, over people. Only about animals. He's started writing to the newspapers, because he can't wait until his next book is published. I asked him, wasn't it better now the Wild Bird Act had been passed, but he said it didn't go far enough. People still eat larks on toast, he said.'

Faith giggled. 'There's more flesh on a pigeon or a partridge. Poor Uncle Joe-Ben! He'll never be happy if he cares so much about things.'

Joe-Ben never thought to ask himself

whether he could claim to be happy. There was more than enough to be done in the world of nature. No sooner was the close season over and the winter nights had begun than the village boys were out with their lamps and nets capturing and killing the birds as they sheltered in the hedgerows. Joe-Ben took to prowling in the darkness, following and attempting to frustrate the purpose of these hunters. So incensed was he with two of the graceless louts that he attacked them physically and to such effect that their fathers threatened an action for assault. It was Rose who managed to smooth matters over.

'You really must curb your temper,' he advised his brother. 'Normally you're such a placid chap, but when you get on your hobby-horse you go berserk.'

'It is not a hobby-horse,' Joe-Ben said, hotly, 'it's a matter of life and death to hundreds of living creatures. And you are no better than those ignorant hobbledehoys. What do I say to you every harvest time? Do you stop the reaper when you reach the centre of the field, and preserve the creatures that are huddled in the last uncut bit of corn? Didn't I see a fox, seven hares and three pheasants, too panic-stricken to move?'

Rose smiled. 'I do admire you, brother, but you know what a waste of time it is to preach to a farmer. You never persuaded Grandfather to have compassion on the animals he killed. He did what he had to do. I'm thankful, though, that I'm faring well enough to be able to dispense with your help. You were not born to be a farmer, however hard you might try to force yourself. Don't bear me any ill-will.'

Joe-Ben shook his head. 'I don't, any more than I can bring myself to hate the stoat that takes the rabbit.'

Often he wondered whether he would ever come to terms with life. It was simpler for Rose. Rose worked hard and did his best for his dependants, as his grandfather had done before him. It had not been easy to make ends meet, but lately his prospects had improved. He had received a visit from a stranger who had put to him an attractive proposition.

Naturally Tirell was the first he told, and for sober, tranquil Rose he was positively excited. 'Mr Fordrough is a dealer in horses, a kind of agent for the London General Omnibus Company, and he is nominating certain small farmers in these parts as suppliers. He says many farmers find it more profitable to breed horses than to plough with them.'

Tirell looked doubtful. 'You mean, change

your method? Get rid of the herd?'

'Perhaps, gradually. Depends how things turn out. You know I'll never make a fortune with cattle. Maybe if I had another couple of hundred acres — '

'Rose, do you really want to make a fortune?'

'I don't know. When I think of Christopher — All that land wasted, employing able-bodied men to plant a lot of buttercups and daisies.'

Tirell burst out laughing. 'Not buttercups and daisies, darling. Exotic things like calceolarias and gloxinias.'

Rose scowled. 'I don't care what their Latin names are. I could do something with that land.'

'You are as bad as Christopher. He wants Farncombes and Marlipins, and you want Marlipins and Farncombes. You are like two greedy children.'

'Please don't compare me with him!'

'Well, then, what of your horses?'

'Mares. The London General uses almost all mares, and they start work at five years old.'

'Gracious! Do we have to wait that long? And what do we use for money?'

Rose's enthusiasm returned. 'We don't wait that long. I shall bring up some youngsters until I can breed my own. As for money, Mr Fordrough has arranged with a finance company to advance what we want. Think, Tirell, they will pay thirty-five pounds for each animal and take all I can produce.'

'All?'

'Yes. London General have about ten thousand horses working, eleven horses allocated to each omnibus.'

Though his family was somewhat sceptical, Rose went ahead, and after three years was beginning to see the project as a steady and profitable business.

With her school Debbie was not so successful. The rebuilt wing was modern and comfortable, yet parents did not clamour to enrol their daughters and the dormitories were rarely full.

'It is the fault of that dreadful Verrall woman,' Debbie stormed.

'Oh, mother!' Constance gazed at her with pity. 'You really are becoming obsessed with Lady Verrall. She will have completely forgotten us by now.'

'I don't believe it,' Debbie insisted. 'Tell me, then, why we find it so difficult to obtain pupils.'

Constance did not know, and there probably was truth in what Debbie said, for mothers had been known to ask, vaguely,

'Wasn't there some trouble at that school? A kind of scandal?'

Sometimes no reply was given, but a person with a longer memory might answer, 'I believe they had a fire, and one of the girls died.'

Then the mothers would shudder and consult the brochures of other schools.

'There is only one thing to do,' Constance said at last, briskly. 'You must cease being so exclusive.'

'Exclusive? I was not aware that I was.'

'Well, you are. Last term you refused a girl because her father was a brewer.'

'Naturally I did. Had he been a director of one of the large companies — This man brewed beer in a shed at the bottom of his garden and sold it in his shop.'

'What about the one whose father was a waste-disposal merchant?'

'He was a rag-and-bone man. Really, Constance, one must draw the line somewhere. When I opened this school I made it a rule not to accept any tradesmen's daughters.'

'Yes, and look where it has left us! With empty beds and empty purses.' Constance's tone was bitter.

Debbie sighed. 'I suppose one will have to lower one's standards. Slightly.'

'If we exclude the parvenus we may as well close the school.'

Debbie gave way because she saw no alternative. She thought, Dear Constance! So sensible!

Constance took charge and inserted advertisements in several midland and northern newspapers, as well as London ones. The response was not overwhelming, but a few ladies undertook the journey to look at the school for themselves. For the most part they were brightly-dressed ladies with unfamiliar accents. They appeared to be impressed by the ancient house and the amount of land surrounding it, and also they were impressed, though they did not show it, by the refined accent of Debbie and her daughters. The schoolmarm and her girls, the ladies decided, were obviously genteel, though it was a pity they were so dowdy, poor souls!

Debbie concealed her distaste and reflected that their money had the same value as that of the gentry, though, to her surprise, they were no more anxious to part with it. 'Do you make a reduction in fees for sisters?' she was asked more than once, and found herself willing to comply. Oh, to have a well-filled classroom once more!

It was during this period of change that Elianor announced her intention of leaving home to take up a career of her own.

Debbie was aghast. 'Leave me? Go away? How shall I run the school?'

'You have Connie and Faith.'

'I have always needed you as well.'

'You don't now. We've scarcely more than half the pupils we had.'

'I know, but they require a great deal more supervision. I cannot understand why it is, perhaps lack of home discipline, but they appear to have no idea that rules must be obeyed.'

'It's the modern way,' Elianor said, lightly. 'What with dress reform and the passion for sport, you simply can't expect girls to be so amenable.'

'What shall I do?' Debbie asked, mournfully. 'The boys have gone, and now you plan to desert me. Soon I shall have no children left at all.'

'You are fortunate to have so large a family. Think of Aunt Dolly with only one son, and Tirell is childless.'

Debbie sighed. 'What do you propose to do?'

'Study hygiene.'

'Hygiene?' Debbie echoed, blankly. 'What is there to study? If you wash your hands frequently and keep your food covered — '

'Oh, mother! I shall take the course

promoted by the National Health Society. I have to have nursing training at a hospital, and cookery classes, and then a special course of hygienic training.'

'I hoped you would all marry and settle down somewhere near me.'

'There is scarcely a wide choice of possible husbands in Brambleden. If Connie and Faith do not make an effort soon, you will have at least two old maids on your hands.'

'How can you put things so crudely, Elianor? If it is the Lord's will that my daughters should marry — '

'I've no idea what the Lord will decide,' Elianor said, bluntly, 'but it certainly is natural to leave home when one is grown up.'

'Sometimes sooner.' Debbie spoke to herself, thinking of the son she had give away, but Elianor mistook her meaning.

'You were fortunate to lose none of us in infancy.'

This time Debbie did not speak aloud. To herself she said, 'But I did! I did!'

2

A man builds a fine house; and now he
has a master, and a task for life.
Ralph Waldo Emerson.

For so long had the building of the house
and the laying out of the gardens occupied
Christopher that it was something in the
nature of a shock to him when he found
himself with nothing to do. Five indoor
servants cooked and cleaned, and a head
gardener and two young assistants kept the
grounds in order. Construction was finished;
all was routine.

He walked through the gardens one day
to the three fields which were a reminder
that the place had been a farm. They looked
untidy and neglected, which, strangely, gave
him a feeling of pleasure. A man could
grow weary, he thought, of neat paths, and
well-trimmed shrubs, and flower-beds where
no blossom dared raise its head higher than
that of its brothers.

He went across the rough grass to the
boundary. Only a hedge and a ditch separated
him from Marlipins land, and he saw that

Rose had laid the nearest field down to oats that year. For the horses, he supposed.

He had heard about those horses. The Half Moon Inn was the great centre of village news, and Rose's venture had been discussed from every angle. The majority of the local people, ultra-conservative as they were, prophesied disaster and seemed almost disappointed when the experiment prospered.

Christopher smiled to himself. He had to grant that Rose was a shrewd fellow. There were times when a change acted like a tonic. Hadn't his father laid the foundations of his fortune when he cleared the cattle from his ranch and went over to sheep? A pity to waste these fields, but what could he do with them? He already had a lake in his grounds, and Dolly had her tennis-court, though she used it little enough.

Horses were pleasant animals, not that he cared for those lumbering creatures Rose bred for pulling omnibuses. But thoroughbreds — race-horses, say.

He remembered his grandfather's downfall and then shrugged off the thought. He was not concerned with gambling. Why should he be, when he had money and to spare? But to be a race-horse owner, that was an occupation for a gentleman.

He rarely shared his ideas and intentions with Dolly, so that it was not surprising she should ask, several weeks later, 'What are those horses doing in the field?'

'Grazing, most likely,' he replied, blandly.

'Are they ours?'

'Well, I can't see myself housing other people's stock. They are rather special, actually. A couple of yearlings I've bought. Some of the best blood in the country. Cost me a mint of money.'

'What are you going to do with them?'

'Race them, obviously.'

'But you don't know anything about racing.'

'What does that matter? It's the trainer's job to look after them and prepare them.'

'So you'll send them away.'

'No, I shall engage a trainer to live here, but first I need more horses, to make it worth his while. I intend to find a first-rate chap, one who knows what's what.'

Dolly looked doubtful. 'You will have to spend a great deal of money.'

'What's wrong with that?'

'Well, the boys will be leaving school in little more than a year. Have you thought about a university?'

Christopher pursed his lips. 'I'm not particularly keen on the idea.'

'Not keen? You were keen enough to get them into Eton.'

'That was different. They had to go to school, so I reckoned they might as well have the best.'

'Then why not carry on with the best, Oxford or Cambridge?'

'My dear girl, do you happen to have read their school reports?'

'Benjy is very bright.'

'But he's no dedicated scholar.'

'He's much more intelligent than Tom is.'

'Oh, yes! You would say that! I suppose you think he gets his brains from that bastard of a bailiff I employed. Well, I shall treat both boys alike, as I've always done. If Tom's not smart enough to get into university, then neither one of them goes.'

'That's not fair.'

Christopher smiled. 'I'll be glad of a couple of strong lads to help with the horses.'

'Benjy's not fond of horses.'

'He likes his pony well enough.'

'That's different. He's used to it, and it's gentle.'

'Young Benjy's a bit of a funk,' Christopher said, contemptuously, 'but I'll see he gets over it.'

Until this conversation Christopher had

not given much thought to the future of the two boys, but now it seemed as though his decision to own and breed racehorses had settled everything satisfactorily. There was no need for either of them to work for a living. The idea of having them at home appealed to him. He had been lonely, he realised, unseated between the two stools of the lower-class villagers he despised and the upper-class local gentry who wished to have nothing to do with him. The boys would be good company, and Tom in time could become his right-hand man.

Once again Farncombes hummed with activity. There were extra stables to be built, and a respectable house for a trainer. Dolly, bewildered, refrained from criticising any of this, for Christopher was much better-tempered when he had something with which to occupy himself.

He engaged a stable-lad called George, a not very prepossessing youth who said he had worked for a well-known trainer, but who was unable to produce a reference. Christopher was willing to waive this formality; he needed a boy who understood horses.

'I'll get a trainer as soon as the house is ready,' he told Dolly. 'With any luck I'll be able to make one or two entries for next year's flat season.'

In the meantime he went to some of the autumn sales, learning what was what, he said, and made one purchase. It was a three-year-old, the rather showy chestnut winner of a selling plate.

'Now you will *have* to engage a trainer,' Dolly said.

He looked sideways at her. Farm managers and horse-trainers, had she an in-built partiality for such fellows? Well, he'd make sure that this one was middle-aged and well and truly married.

'Plenty of time,' he said. 'George can manage until I increase my stock.'

When the boys arrived home for the Christmas holidays Christopher's first procedure was to take them to the stables.

'I'm a race-horse owner now,' he told them. 'That'll be something to make the local gentry sit up and take notice. Just you wait until I've had a Derby winner!'

The boys dutifully admired the yearlings and then Christopher led them to a door over which was the name 'Corporal Violet.'

'This one has already proved himself. Take him out, George.'

The stable-lad moved forward, and as he did so there came a tremendous banging and thumping.

'He's trying to kick down the door, that's

all,' George said, apologetically.

Tom's eyes were round with wonder. 'Does he often do that?'

George winked. 'Only when he feels restive, which is generally. But I can manage him.'

Benjy had moved back, well behind Christopher.

Christopher turned and glanced at him. 'You'll have to grow used to horses. There's going to be a whole lot of 'em around here. George can teach you a thing or two about them, can't you, George? Anyway, we'll leave the Corporal now until he's quietened down.'

Benjy heaved a sigh of relief and took a step or two forward. 'That's a funny name. What does it mean?'

'The owner said it was what they called Napoleon, who told his friends he'd get back from Elba when the violets were in bloom.'

Benjy nodded. 'I see. He was called the petit caporal too.'

Christopher laughed. 'Nothing petty about this one. He's a great strong brute.'

When the boys were alone Benjy confided to Tom, 'I don't like horses.'

'Don't be silly! You like Barclay.'

'He's different. He's small, and he doesn't kick his stable door.'

'They are getting too small for us.'

'Not for me.'

For several years the boys had had their own ponies which they rode in the holidays. They called them Barclay and Perkins, which Christopher thought amusing and original, though Dolly was not so sure.

'Fancy naming ponies after a brewery! People will imagine we are tipplers.'

'Well, they know that sometimes I'm none the better for what I take,' Christopher admitted.

'All the same — '

All the same the names stuck, and the boys were devoted to their ponies, so that it was a shock when a few days after Christmas they discovered the animals were missing.

'What have you done with them?' Benjy demanded of George.

'I ain't done nothing.'

'Where are they, then?'

'Better ask your father.'

They went straight to Christopher. 'What's happened to Barclay and Perkins?'

Christopher answered blandly. 'Ah! I was going to tell you. I've sold them.'

The boys were dumbfounded. Had Benjy been two or three years younger he would have burst into tears. As it was, a lump rose into his throat, his eyes smarted and his fists clenched. At that moment he hated

Christopher, and the silent prayer flashed through his mind. 'Oh, God, strike him dead!'

Tom was sad and sorry, but his emotion was in no way comparable with Benjy's. He knew he was getting too heavy for Perkins, and it was cruel to overweight a horse. The ponies would be far happier carrying children.

'Did you want the beasts to collapse under you?' Christopher demanded.

Benjy found his voice. 'Barclay wouldn't, under me. I'm barely eight stone. I could have ridden him for years. I could have ridden him for always. Why didn't you tell us what you were going to do?'

'I don't have to consult you as to my actions,' Christopher said, coldly. He was studying Benjy closely. 'You're quite right. Funny I never noticed before. You are a bit of a runt.'

'I'm not. I'm just light.'

'That as well. A spindle-shanks. Not much to cover your skeleton.'

The words hurt more than a whip. A beating he could take, but to realise that Christopher so despised him was wellnigh unbearable.

Tom understood a little of what Benjy was feeling. 'Everybody doesn't have to be big,' he said. 'Elephants are big but cheetahs are fast.'

Christopher nodded approval. 'Quite right, my son. Small men have their uses too. Time we planned Benjy's future. Yours, also. What do you want to do, Benjy?'

At that moment Benjy wanted only to be alone, probably to be sick. 'I — I suppose we'll go to Oxford,' he stammered.

'No. No, I don't think that will be necessary.'

'But — '

'You're neither of you very brainy.'

'I'd work hard,' Benjy promised.

'And what would you do after you left university?'

'I'd like to be a reporter on a newspaper.'

'Why, that's not particularly ambitious. Perhaps you've forgotten that you don't have to work for a living. I have sufficient money to keep all of us.'

'I'd rather earn my own,' Benjy said, stubbornly.

'Well, that's a desirable sentiment. As a matter of fact I have plans for you.'

The tension went out of Benjy, leaving him weak but sparked with hope. 'Could I please have Barclay back, then? I won't get any heavier. I could easily eat less.'

'I'm afraid it's too late for that. People

won't return goods they have bought.'

The hope faded, yet there was pleasure and gratitude in the fact that Christopher had praised him. A desirable sentiment. That was praise, wasn't it? And to have plans for him, wasn't that a sign that Christopher loved him, not as much as he loved Tom, of course, but, still, love was love?

'You're the right build for a jockey,' Christopher went on. 'Don't know why I didn't think of it before. Tomorrow I'll get George to put you up on Corporal Violet.'

There was not time to be alone. Benjy's stomach rose against him. He was sick then and there, right in front of Christopher.

3

Never yet was a springtime
When the buds forgot to blow.
Margaret Elizabeth Sangster

The best anyone could have said concerning Constance Aylwin's appearance was that it was pleasant. Most people would have described her as 'homely', and with this her mother would have been inclined to agree. Yet if Debbie had been forced to choose a favourite daughter — a most misguided thing to do — Constance would have been that one. Constance, like the majority of Rose's horses, was good-tempered, strong and willing. She rarely complained about anything, and Debbie found her an abiding comfort in adversity.

The school had never really recovered from the damaging publicity of the fire, and Debbie found herself accepting, not only pupils of a lower social order, but also a few day girls, daughters of local farmers. Inwardly she might shudder at this altered aspect of her academy, but Constance seemed not to notice the difference.

Constance it was who increased the time devoted to sport, after her mother had been convinced of its benefits.

'Hockey?' Debbie had demurred. 'Surely that is a game for men, not for young ladies.'

'It was, but now it is becoming very popular with girls. Several ladies' hockey clubs have been formed in London. We should have a softer ball than men use, a tennis ball, I think.'

'I should hope so. We don't wish to see our pupils in hospital.'

'It provides a game for winter, when we can no longer play lawn tennis or cricket.'

'Well — '

'Besides, it makes the girls pleasantly tired. Haven't you noticed, mother, that their behaviour is better when they have had exercise?'

Debbie had noticed, and gave way. She even came to welcome the sound of the clash of hockey-sticks, and the screams of the more excitable girls. Maintaining discipline, she had discovered, was more difficult among the class of girls she now received. Or was it the general trend of modern life? There seemed to be a lamentable increase in the liberties taken by females. Dear Constance! What a tower of strength she was!

Not so frequently did Debbie murmur 'Dear Faith!' to herself. Faith, she supposed, was the beauty of the family. Certainly she was extremely pretty. Yes, and extremely lazy and self-willed. Added to which, she hobnobbed far too much with the pupils.

'You should keep your distance,' her mother advised. 'Unless you hold yourself aloof you will never earn their respect.'

Faith shrugged her shoulders. 'Why should I? Who wants respect anyway? They like me well enough.'

'You are not here to be liked.' Debbie's voice was stern. 'The question is, do they obey you?' Faith's laugh had a sound of insolence, and Debbie went on, angrily, 'You are supposed to set an example. You'll do no good for yourself by mixing with a girl like Beatrice Luff.'

'Oh, Beatie's all right. She's older than the others.'

'Yes, and we know why, don't we? It is because she is so backward with her studies. Her mother sent her to us as a last hope.' Debbie's tone was bitter.

'I don't care,' Faith said, sulkily. 'She's good fun. It's little enough amusement we get.'

'When your Aunt Dolly and I were girls,' her mother told her, 'we found amusement in our work. I'm sure I don't know what kind of fun you want.'

Faith looked at her with pity. No, she wouldn't know what kind of fun young girls wanted. But Faith knew. She wanted to wear pretty clothes and meet young men. She was sick of the all-female company in which she spent most of her time, sick of a household in which she saw no men except elderly ones like Uncle Joe-Ben and Uncle Rose. Beatie was three years younger than Faith, yet she could tell quite scandalous tales of her encounters with the opposite sex.

'Stuck in this dead-alive hole you'll never know nothing about men,' Beatrice prophesied. 'Mark my words, you'll end up an old maid.'

'No, I won't.' Faith was offended, but she could think of no reply except, 'My mother didn't.'

Beatrice laughed. 'Who did she marry, eh? The village schoolmaster, wasn't it?'

'You won't find anybody better.'

'Oh, yes, I will. None of your chaw-bacons for me. We get the swells coming down to Brighton. You should see the church parade on Hove lawns Sunday morning. Real toffs they are.'

'I wish I could see them,' Faith said, wistfully.

There was no compassion in Beatrice. 'Don't suppose you ever will. Ooh, I just can't wait for the holidays. Think of me on Easter Sunday.'

But she was to be disappointed. There came a letter from her mother announcing that she was taking a trip abroad, and would kind Mrs Aylwin keep Beatrice at school during these holidays?

Debbie did not feel particularly kind about the matter, but she was not in a position to antagonise any pupils' parents, and certainly the extra money would come in useful.

'What on earth shall we do with the child?' Debbie asked her daughters.

'I will set her some holiday tasks,' Constance promised. 'I think Sir Walter Scott would occupy her pleasantly. Do you advise 'Kenilworth'? Or perhaps 'Tales of my Landlord' would be better. After all, it does run into several volumes.'

Faith laughed. 'I don't believe Beatie would thank you for any of them. It will be the holidays, wherever she is. She'll expect to be entertained.'

Her mother sighed. 'Oh, my goodness! How does one entertain a girl of that age? Especially one of rather — well, plebeian tastes.'

'I'll take her out,' Faith volunteered.

'Now you know I don't approve of — '

'It might be convenient,' Constance suggested, gently. 'Since Beatrice will be with us and we cannot escape her — She seems to have taken a fancy to Faith, and Faith is nearer her age — '

Faith sniffed. 'Don't be so priggish! You're only a year older than I am.'

'But she is a great deal more sensible,' Debbie told her, sharply. 'I suppose it will do no harm to accompany the girl on a walk now and again. It will keep her out of mischief, and prevent her from becoming bored.'

Beatrice had every intention of avoiding boredom, if it were at all possible. Disappointed she was at missing the diversions of her Brighton home, yet she felt that somewhere in this dead-alive place amusement was to be found.

First she tried the farm. Cows and pigs and poultry were, in her opinion, useless until they were cooked and on the table, but there was something rather fascinating about the fine stout horses Rose was breeding.

She begged him to give her a ride on one of them, and obligingly he lifted her up. This he did several times, as a favour to Debbie, but when it became a daily occurrence he rebelled.

'Listen, miss, these are not riding-horses. If you want excitement you had better go next-door, to Farncombes. There they have racehorses.'

Beatrice pouted. She was not much of a horsewoman, and mostly she had enjoyed being picked up in the arms of a man — an older man, it is true, but strong and quite good-looking.

To Faith she said, 'Your Uncle Rose is not much fun. Everyone is so dull around here. There must be *something* amusing we can do.'

Faith racked her brains. Yes, surely there must be something. 'There's church on Sundays — '

'Church! Do you call that amusing?'

'Well, it's nice wearing our best clothes, and seeing all the people. Then there's market, but that's mostly for men. And there's the fairs.'

'Fairs?'

'Yes. Next week is Brambleden Spring Fair.'

'That sounds more promising.'

'We never go, though.'

'Never go? Whyever not?'

'Mother thinks the pupils' parents would disapprove. You get a lot of rough people there, gipsies and so on.'

'Oh, I'd like that. Anyway, there aren't any pupils here now.'

'You're one.'

'No, I'm not, not really. You don't have pupils in the holidays. Ask your mother if we can go.'

Faith asked, and found her mother difficult to persuade. 'It is not an occasion for well-brought-up young ladies.'

'Oh, mother, you sound more like a schoolmistress every day.'

'I am a schoolmistress.'

'Still there's no need to sound like one,' Faith insisted, with rather shaky logic. 'We need some buttons and pins and needles, and Beatie has broken her comb.'

In the end Debbie gave way, with the strict injunction that they should visit the fair early in the day and return well before sundown.

At first Beatrice found it enjoyable. They went from stall to stall, Beatrice spending a considerable amount of the money with which she was always well supplied. They threw balls at Aunt Sally and at coconuts, and visited several dubious freaks shrouded in tents.

Then Beatrice said, 'Is that all?'

'Yes.'

'I don't think much of it. As for rough

people, these are as respectable as church-wardens.'

'Oh, that comes later.'

Beatrice pricked up her ears. 'What do you mean?'

'Only that evening gets a bit wild.' Faith wished she hadn't mentioned it, for Beatrice immediately determined to return to the fair. 'I shall have a headache,' she said, 'and go to bed very early.'

'How do you imagine I shall get out?'

'You'll have to think of something,' Beatrice told her, airily, 'otherwise I'll go alone.'

Faith was torn between two responsibilities, that of obeying her mother, and that of guarding the wayward Beatrice. Eventually, after taking Beatrice soothing drinks for her imaginary headache, she announced that she too was rather tired and would go to bed.

Stealthily the girls crept out and away down the road towards the glow in the sky which marked the centre of the village and the fair. Though the more circumspect of the villagers had departed to their homes and a good night's rest, the festivities were by no means over. Sporadic fireworks were being let off, and on the green young people were dancing to music supplied by a violin and a clarinet.

'This is better,' Beatrice said. 'Let's dance.'

'I don't know the steps.'

'What do steps matter? These bumpkins don't know any more steps than the cows they milk. Let's dance together until we find a couple of boys.'

'Oh, Beatie, I don't think — '

Beatrice nudged her. 'What are they doing?'

Reluctantly Faith explained. 'This is what they call dragging-time, when the boys begin pulling the girls about.'

As she spoke two youths approached, grabbed the arms of the girls and separated them. Faith struggled, but the boy was strong and already Beatrice was out of sight.

'You don't want to be contrairy,' the boy said.

Faith knew him slightly. He was Caleb Stower, son of a local farmer, and vaguely she supposed this made her escapade slightly less reprehensible than it might have been.

But quickly he tired of dancing and began to walk away off the green, pulling Faith behind him.

'Let me go!' she panted.

'Oh, quit your squacketting!'

'I shall scream.'

He laughed. 'Think you'll be heard in all this racket?'

He strode ahead quickly, still holding her arm, so that she almost had to run, and did not stop until they were away from the houses and in a field.

Behind the hedge he threw himself to the ground and pulled her down. 'This is where we have fun.'

'You won't — you won't do anything, will you?' she asked pleadingly.

'No more than what the fellows and girls most always do.'

'Do you know who I am?'

'You're a village wench.'

'I'm Faith Aylwin. My mother has the school at Marlipins.'

He guffawed. 'Well, I reckon as I can learn you some things you never was taught at school.'

He began to pull up her skirts, and she fought him with all her strength. 'Don't hurt me!' she begged.

He did hurt her, but he was not brutal, and before it was over she had ceased to resist, had almost gone towards him, had begun to want.

4

Corporal Violet

The thought of the Easter holidays was with Benjy all through that school term. Whether he was at lessons or at sport it was as though he carried a heavy burden and could not put it down. The days grew longer and the cold grew stronger, and Benjy wanted time to stop; but there came a softness in the air and a smell of live earth, and he knew nothing could delay his return to Farncombes and what awaited him there.

It might have helped if he could have told Tom about it, but this was the one thing he could not share, which was measure of its gravity. Throughout their childhood Benjy had craved not only Tom's love but his respect, and still it was a matter of prime importance to him. Should Tom come to despise him, Benjy believed life would be unendurable. Only he himself knew what he had suffered in attempts to prove himself as brave as Tom, though there were some things that could not be concealed. The fear of loud noises, such as fireworks, was one of these, but mercifully Tom had devised his own explanation, and so Benjy's courage was not in question.

'I expect you've got weak ears,' said matter-of-fact Tom.

'Weak what?'

'Ears. Well, some people have weak eyes and can't see so well. Reckon you've got weak ears, so noises hurt them.'

Benjy's gratitude was boundless. Tom had provided him with an honourable excuse. He no longer needed to feel ashamed.

The horse was a different matter. Benjy made no protest the first time they hoisted him into the saddle, but as he looked down, it was as if from a precipice, and his bowels turned to water. Corporal Violet, ill-tempered and badly trained, prepared after his fashion to relieve himself of his unwelcome rider. Benjy felt the tensing of the powerful muscles and realised he had never before known real terror. It was almost a relief to fly through the air and hit the ground.

He was not injured, but when they picked him up he was shaking so uncontrollably that he pretended to be slightly hurt. How else could he account for the state in which they found him?

Had this been a single incident, his one and only attempt to ride the horse, it might have made less impression on him, but he had been promised a repetition, or, rather, a number of repetitions.

Christopher said, heartily, 'Never mind. Just wait for Easter holidays. Weather'll be better then, and you can take the animal out every day, like the real apprentices do.'

It was a frightful prospect, a haunting which robbed the term of all its pleasure and left Benjy drained and dispirited.

Dolly was dismayed at the sight of him. 'Why, I do believe you are thinner than ever. Do they give you anything to eat at that place?'

'Of course they do! Plenty.'

'Well, you don't look like it. I'm going to feed you up.'

'You'll do nothing of the kind,' Christopher told her, sharply.

'I shall. I shall give him good big meals. If I can't feed my own son — '

Christopher glared at her. 'A jockey needs to be small and light.'

She snorted. 'A jockey? Whoever heard such nonsense? Benjy will never make a jockey.'

For an instant Benjy knew a flicker of hope, but Christopher soon extinguished it. 'That's what he wants to be, and he shall have what he wants. You want to be a jockey, eh, son?'

Benjy thought he saw pleading in Christopher's eyes, and suddenly he realised that here was a disappointed man, a sad man. How could he deny him? He believed Christopher to be his father, but Christopher rarely called him 'son'. The word brought a warmth to his heart.

That night Benjy could not sleep. Desperately he longed to please Christopher, but he knew that to do so he would have to become a jockey, have to prove himself in ways that were foreign to him and terrible to contemplate. Surely, he thought, he could do it. They said a man could do anything he wanted to, if he wanted it badly enough. He thought of himself in a silk shirt decorated with Farncombe colours, thundering past a winning post, and a smiling Christopher waiting to lead him in. But across the picture came another one, of Corporal Violet waiting in his stable, beating a tattoo with his hooves on the door, exposing his yellow teeth in an equine grin.

Tom heard him tossing and turning. 'You don't really want to be a jockey, do you, Benjy?'

'I do. I want to do what Father wants. We both want to do that. You do, don't you?'

'Not if it's different from what I want,' Tom replied, practically.

Benjy sighed. 'You don't have to worry. If you were a jockey you'd have to ride one of Uncle Rose's omnibus horses.'

The idea was funny. Tom laughed, relieved. If Benjy could make a joke he couldn't be feeling too badly about his riding. All the same, it could do no harm, he thought, if he spoke to Christopher.

'Aren't you going to engage a trainer, Father?'

'I have done,' Christopher answered, 'but he won't be free until next month.'

'Then why not wait until then to put Benjy on that horse?'

'I expect you'll both be back at school before the man arrives.'

'There are the summer holidays.'

'You'll have left. Next term will be your last. Had you forgotten? I hope you've decided what you want to do.'

Tom was not to be sidetracked. 'That boy George is a fool. He has no idea of controlling the horse.'

'Oh, Corporal Violet is all right. He's not vicious, only high-spirited.'

'He'll throw Benjy again.'

'What of it? If a jockey can't get used to a few falls, he's no good.'

There was little more to be said. Tom looked at the man he believed to be his father, and thought, I hate him. It's wrong to hate your father, but I do. He's cruel and selfish. He doesn't care for anyone, only for getting his own way.

Benjy walked to the stables on feet of lead. George was waiting with the horse, and as Benjy passed, it snapped at his arm. 'He be playful this morning,' George said. 'Do 'ee want to mount him here, Master Benjy?'

'No. Bring him to the field.'

Benjy hoped he did not sound as nervous as he felt. He was anxious for the softness of the damp turf. If he must bite the ground, let it be the grass he bit. Christopher had had the stables built of stone, with a blue-brick yard on which the iron-shod hooves rang as if on an anvil.

That day Benjy did not fall off, but the next day he did, and the one after that. In ten days he was thrown six times.

'Are you feeling better?' Tom wanted to know.

'What do you mean, feeling better?' Benjy asked, crossly. 'I feel fine.'

'I mean, are you getting the hang of staying on the horse?'

Benjy did not care for the wording of the

question. 'I shall soon master him,' he said, carelessly.

Tom looked at him with pity, but knew better than to express his concern. Benjy had his pride, like everyone else.

To Christopher Tom suggested, 'Why don't you let me ride Corporal Violet?'

'You?' Christopher was surprised. 'Don't suppose you could.'

'As well as Benjy does.'

'You're too heavy.'

Tom bit back the, 'Don't be silly!' he wanted to say, because it sounded disrespectful. Instead he said, 'That horse could carry an elephant.'

Christopher had not considered putting Tom on Corporal Violet, but now that he did, he knew he did not like the idea.

'It wouldn't be safe,' he said, without thinking.

'Is it safe for Benjy, then?'

There was no answer to this, but Christopher had to find one. He could scarcely confess, 'You matter to me. Benjy doesn't — not so much. Benjy, the byblow of my farm manager.' He could only mumble, 'Benjy's light. You'd fall heavy. Break your bones.'

On the eleventh day Christopher said to Benjy, 'You're improving.' It was true that on the previous morning Benjy had not fallen. 'I want you to mount here.'

Benjy's heart sank. 'Here?'

'Yes. Can't lead the animal out for ever. You must take full charge.'

Benjy contemplated a blank refusal, but that would take even more courage than obedience. After all, he was used to obeying Christopher, and George's hands were cupped ready for him to mount.

He was getting used to the height from the ground, which had seemed so alarming after the cosy size of Barclay. He was even able to endure calmly the gathering together of the horse's muscles, but he knew he would never learn to predict Corporal Violet's intentions.

That morning the horse sensed the change in routine. Here he was with the rider on his back, instead of being led through the gate and down the lane to the field. Here he was, free and at liberty, for the boy on his back scarcely counted as anything, and the hands on the reins were not those of one who must be obeyed.

As a preliminary Corporal Violet half reared and then circled the yard, quite slowly, at a trot.

Christopher, Tom and George moved back, out of the way of the animal.

'He's doing better,' Christopher said.

Tom did not know whether he meant

140

Benjy or the horse, and there was no time to find out, for, having found that he could please himself, the horse circled the yard again, this time breaking into a canter.

Benjy tried to pull him up, so that someone might open the gate, but Corporal Violet had other ideas. He made no effort to slow down, but, to the astonishment of Benjy and those watching, he galloped madly across the yard and jumped the gate.

Had Benjy been prepared he might have stuck on; as it was he had no chance. When the horse's forequarters rose, Benjy slipped backwards. The horse cleared the gate, and Benjy crashed into the yard, falling on the bricks.

Christopher and Tom reached him at the same time. He was lying on his back, his eyes open, conscious.

'Are you all right, boy?' Christopher bent down. 'Come on, boy! I'll help you up.'

At the same time Tom cried, 'No! Leave him!'

'What do you mean, leave him?' Christopher spoke crossly. Tom was in his way.

Tom ignored him. 'Are you hurt, Benjy?'

'I don't know. It's my back, I think. I can't move.'

'He'll be all right. I'll carry him into the house.'

'No. We shouldn't touch him.'

'What! Leave him here in the cold?'

'We'll cover him with a blanket and get the doctor.'

'Don't be a fool! He's been thrown plenty of times. You'll be all right, won't you, Benjy? I'll carry him in and we'll make him comfortable.'

Tom was standing over Benjy, straddling him. 'You're not to move him. It's dangerous.'

Christopher was angry, and when he was angry he didn't stop to think. 'Don't you tell me what to do! I know what's best.' Tom stayed where he was. 'Get off!' Christopher shouted, and shouldered him roughly aside.

He bent down and lifted Benjy. He did so as gently as possible, but Benjy screamed once and then lapsed into unconsciousness.

5

A day after the fair.
John Heywood.

Beatrice Luff was not aware of possessing a conscience. Limbs could be seen, and some internal organs occasionally felt, but to her the reality of conscience equalled that of fairies and hobgoblins.

So on the morning after her escapade with Faith she was congratulating herself on their having returned to the house and their beds without being heard.

'Nobody knows and nobody'll ever know,' she said. 'Wasn't it fun?'

Faith did not look as though she had had fun. Her face was glum. 'We should never have gone. It was a wicked thing to do.'

'What's it matter?' Beatrice took a brandy-ball from a paper-bag and popped it in her mouth. 'Have one? They're rather stuck together.' Faith shook her head. 'I like doing wicked things,' Beatrice went on, licking her fingers. 'I bet Madame Aylwin would be furious if she knew.'

'Don't call her that!'

143

'All the girls do.'

'Not to me they don't. They have more respect because she's my mother.'

'Well, anyway, she'll never know, so it's all right.'

'That doesn't make it all right,' Faith argued. 'It's on my conscience. Isn't it on yours?'

Beatrice sighed. People asked such difficult questions. 'I don't believe so,' she admitted. 'I can't feel anything. Maybe I haven't a conscience.'

'Don't be silly! Everyone has one. We're born with them.'

'Perhaps mine doesn't work, then.'

Faith could find no answer to this, and after a little hesitation she asked, 'Beatie, what did you do when — when, you know, you danced with that boy?'

'We danced.'

'Nothing else?'

'Oh, we went off and lay in the bushes. What about you?'

'The same.' Faith had a longing to confess everything, but she was afraid. In spite of her sophistication Beatrice was only a kid, and, besides, Faith did not altogether trust her. She hesitated, then asked, 'Did you do anything?'

'Yes. He kissed me, and we played about.

Is something the matter, Faith? You've gone so pale.'

'It's nothing,' Faith told her, hastily. 'I'm just tired, being up so late.'

She tried to convince herself that her secret was safe. Caleb Stower would not mention it, for fear of getting into trouble himself. Yet she knew too well that little remained hidden in Brambleden. Someone might have recognised her, have seen Caleb dragging her away. Each morning she watched her mother's face for some sign, waited for her to speak the words which would show she had heard rumours.

Several days later, when she went down to breakfast, she thought the worst had happened. Debbie was obviously upset. Her expression was grim. Faith's heart missed a beat. The room swam before her eyes, and she felt as if she would faint.

But when her mother spoke, the news had nothing to do with Faith or the Cuckoo Fair.

'There has been an accident at Farncombes. Benjy was thrown from a horse.'

'Was he hurt?'

'Yes. It may be serious.' Debbie sighed. 'You know what village gossip is, but apparently two or three doctors were sent for, from London.'

Faith was weak with relief. Her legs under the table trembled so much that she put her hands on her thighs to still them. Now the village had something else to talk about. It was providential. She could almost be glad of the accident.

So that no one should notice anything strange about her, she asked, as calmly as she could, 'Why didn't they have Aunt Tirell?'

Debbie snorted. 'That will be Christopher's doing. Your Aunt Dolly would have wanted her. After all, Tirell brought Benjy into the world. I think I must go over to Farncombes.'

Constance stared at her. 'But you never visit them. There's a family feud, isn't there?'

'Don't exaggerate! Feud, indeed! There has been nothing more than a few differences of opinion, and if I did not go to my twin sister when she was in trouble, I should despise myself.'

All the same, it was with nervousness that Debbie approached the massive house. If she could have entered by a back door and gone straight to Dolly — But she had no right to do that. She had to walk the length of the gravelled drive — and what a long length it was — like any casual visitor, and knock on the heavy door, a fake imitation of the good, solid ancient door of Marlipins.

She was not surprised when a dignified elderly butler opened the door, but she was extremely annoyed when he declined to show her in.

'I fully realise the family is suffering under severe strain,' she told him, 'and that visitors are not being received. But I am Mrs Waldron's sister.'

The butler was unimpressed. In his opinion relatives could spell trouble, especially when they had not come to the house previously.

Debbie was about to turn away, furious, when Tom came to her rescue and insisted she should be shown in.

'I'm sorry,' he said, 'but everything is rather upset at present.'

Her first impression of him was that he had suddenly become older. He was a young man now, not a boy, and a splendid young man. Even Bertram and Bysshe could not compare with him. Her heart swelled until it seemed to fill her whole body, and she yearned as never before to claim him her son.

'I'll tell Mother you called,' he said, gravely, 'but I can't just now. The doctor has given her a sleeping-draught. She's not slept for nights. She wouldn't leave Benjy.'

'How is he?'

'The doctors say he will live.'

'Is it — is it as bad as that?'

'Yes. The spinal cord has been injured.' He spoke calmly, but she could sense the tension in him, the withholding of some violent emotion. It was the grief and anxiety for Benjy, of course, but there was something more. She could see it in his eyes, a rage which scarcely could be kept from boiling over.

'Tom,' she said, 'Tom, you mustn't let it tear you apart.'

'You don't understand.' He spoke stiffly.

'I do. I understand everything about you. I . . . '

She did not know what she would have said, but that was the moment when Christopher entered the room.

He looked at Debbie and demanded, 'What are you doing here?'

Tom replied for her. 'She came to see Mother,' and Christopher relaxed. There had been a moment of panic, wondering what Debbie had said to the boy.

'All right,' he said, 'you can run away now. I want to talk to your Aunt Debbie.'

An innate sense of politeness, and years of the necessity for tact made Debbie wait until the door closed behind Tom, and then she demanded, 'Why the pretence? Why the 'Aunt Debbie'? Isn't it time you told Ninian the truth?'

'Not Ninian,' Christopher said, mechanically, 'Tom.'

'He was christened Ninian, after his father.'

Christopher took a step towards Debbie. 'I am his father, and I won't have you coming here making trouble.'

She thought he might strike her or shake her, but she did not flinch. Poor Dolly, she thought, poor Dolly who was foolish but certainly did not deserve Christopher.

'Sooner or later my son must know the truth.'

'Then it had better be later. A fine thing for your reputation,' Christopher jeered, 'a fine thing for your school and your family, to hear that I was your lover.'

'Not my lover, my rapist.'

'Who would believe that?'

'Those who know me, and those who know what my husband was to me, they would believe. You must be mad, Christopher, to suppose you can keep Ninian in ignorance. He is practically a man. He'll be leaving school this summer, won't he? Will you shut him up, make a hermit of him? How else can you prevent people from talking, prevent him from hearing? Someone is bound to tell him that you and Dolly adopted him.'

'That will be pleasant for you,' Christopher

jeered. 'The schoolmarm who gave away her bastard son.'

Debbie looked at him steadily. 'I could kill you, but I came here to commiserate with Dolly. Have you no concern for Benjy?'

Christopher shrugged his shoulders. 'Sorry about the accident, of course. I was hoping to make a jockey of the boy, but it looks as though he's going to disappoint me.'

His tone of calm indifference infuriated her. 'You don't mean — '

'Well, what's the good, if he can't stick on a horse?'

'But he'll recover?'

'They don't know. There are more tests to be taken. I guess we'll just have to wait and see. I've had the best medical advice, you know, two fellows from London, real top-notchers. I always give the boys the best of everything.'

'Yes,' Debbie agreed, bitterly, 'the best that money will buy,' and she turned and left him, left the house without waiting to be shown out.

To her mother she said, 'The older he grows the more insufferable Christopher becomes.'

Alice sighed. 'I wish we could do something to help Dolly. The whole village is talking about Christopher's new scheme. They say

150

he aims to have the largest racing stables in the country.'

'Oh, yes! He must always have the largest of everything. But I have had enough of him. I swear I'll never set foot in Farncombes again.'

Alice looked sideways at her. 'Not even to see Ninian?'

Debbie's eyes filled with tears. 'Oh, mother, he's such a fine young man. I'm so proud of him, and — '

She turned away, unable to say more. It was no use regretting the past, she thought, drearily, no use blaming oneself for one's mistakes. She should be thankful that two of her children were still with her and likely to be the comfort of her old age. Constance was a true home-lover, and Faith seemed to be settling down nicely.

Had she been aware of Faith's state of mind she would have been considerably less composed.

From being uneasy Faith was becoming frightened. Desperately she longed to confide in someone, and could think of no one except Beatrice. Since their visit to the Cuckoo Fair the friendship between the two girls had cooled. Faith was not quite sure why it was, but she felt it had something to do with her experience with Caleb Stower. She had found

it impossible to tell Beatrice about this, but
now it seemed she had no alternative. She
needed advice from the younger girl.

To her surprise Beatrice was in her room
packing. 'Why are you in such a hurry? You
don't go until the day after tomorrow.'

Beatrice smoothed and folded a lace-edged
petticoat. 'I've a lot to do.'

Faith looked at the two large leather
trunks. 'I suppose you have.' She sighed.
'Lucky you!'

'Besides,' Beatrice went on, 'I'll be glad to
get home. This is a dead-alive place.'

Faith had a prick of envy. 'We had a
good time at the fair,' she reminded her,
defensively.

'Oh, that! That was weeks ago.'

'Six weeks. Beatie, I wanted to ask you
something. I don't suppose it's anything, but
I'm a tiny bit worried. It's — it's the curse.
I haven't had it.'

Beatrice straightened up and looked search-
ingly at her. 'When were you due?'

'About a fortnight after. I didn't think
anything of it. I mean, I reckoned I was
just going to be late. But now I think I'm
going to miss again.'

'What happened with that boy?'

'Well, you know.'

'You mean you did it properly?'

152

'I guess so. Beatie, what do you think?'

'I think you're a fool.'

Faith stared at her. 'Is that all? Is that all you can say? Beatie, I'm frightened. You must help me.'

'Me? What can I do?'

'Something. There must be something. You told me about all the men you've been out with, and — and how you carried on.'

'Maybe I did,' Beatrice said, scornfully, 'but I didn't expect you to act like an utter idiot. You don't suppose, do you, that I'd let a man get me into trouble?'

Faith's heart sank. Trouble. That was the word they used, the terrifying word. Was it possible that she was in trouble? 'Is that all you can say?' she repeated, pathetically.

'No.' Beatrice shut the lid of her trunk with a bang. 'What I say is you've got to know what's o'clock to keep out of trouble, and I'll be main glad to be back in Brighton.'

6

I loved her for that she was beautiful.
Philip James Bailey.

There had been some doubt as to whether Tom should return to Eton for his last term. With Benjy confined to his bed and his complete recovery still uncertain, a few more weeks of education for Tom became of minor importance, but finally Dolly and Christopher agreed that he should go back.

Dolly was glad of the opportunity to have Benjy to herself. So inseparable were the two boys that she had felt left out, slightly jealous of their devotion, and now, with Benjy helpless, she could care for him, be a real mother. It would give her a purpose in life.

Christopher also welcomed the chance to get his stables in working condition. He wanted Tom, when he came home from school, to find a career ready and waiting for him. The trainer, Matthew Cruttenden, seemed a reliable and enterprising man. Christopher consented to his engaging an assistant as well as the boy George, and declared himself willing to take on a

154

couple of apprentices as soon as they had sufficient bloodstock to warrant it. Meanwhile he bought three two-year-old horses and two well-bred brood mares, and beside the elaborate wrought-iron gates erected a large board on which was inscribed The Farncombe Stud.

These activities gave the village a great deal to talk about, and considerable room for exaggeration. Someone got the idea that Christopher was building a race-course in his grounds, and one of the locals went so far as to prophesy they'd soon be running the Derby at Brambleden.

At Marlipins they were not impressed. 'That Christopher!' Rose said, disgustedly. 'He's just a showoff. I might as well put up a placard advertising The London General Omnibus Stud.'

Tirell chuckled. 'Why not? That would give the villagers even more pleasure. They are humming like a hive of bees, and it's three weeks since Mrs Pyefinch sent for me in the middle of the night.'

Mrs Pyefinch was Brambleden's oldest inhabitant. She would be one hundred on November the thirtieth, and was determined that nothing should mar the day.

'Well, if we have Christopher to thank for Mrs Pyefinch being prevented from suffering a rising of the lights, then good luck to him!'

Tirell nodded. 'We shouldn't make fun of him. He's had a bad blow. The poor man must feel very guilty about Benjy's accident.'

Rose was not so sympathetic. He had known Christopher longer than she had. 'A blow to his pride, yes. Ninian — I should say Tom, I suppose — will be home for good soon. I wonder what Christopher's plans are for him.'

'Daisy, too,' Tirell reminded him. 'She'll have finished school.'

'Why, so she will!' He was surprised. 'How time flies! I hope Joe-Ben — '

He broke off, because he was not sure quite what he hoped for or from Joe-Ben, but Tirell understood.

Joe-Ben had not considered the ending of Daisy's schooldays. Indeed, when she was away the thought of her rarely entered his mind. He felt no guilt on this account, for he was convinced he had done his best for her. Each term he cheerfully paid the fees which Debbie maintained were exorbitant, and during each vacation he made no complaint about handing over whatever sum of money was required for providing Daisy with the wardrobe suitable for a young lady at a finishing school. It was simply that he did not feel Daisy belonged to him. The fact that she had cost Joan her life was something he could never forget, and to expect him to find in her a replica of his dead darling was, he thought, pure rubbish.

As far as he could see, Madame de Valmore's establishment had had little or no beneficial effect. Daisy had always been a reserved child, and now she was a reserved and decidedly affected young lady. She spoke with a refined accent, used long words and gave herself airs.

Debbie, only too glad to be able to point out that a Swiss finishing school was no Utopia, went to Joe-Ben with the news that she had caught Daisy smoking cigarettes. 'Disgraceful!' She exclaimed. 'Had she been one of my daughters or one of my pupils I would have had her over my knee and thoroughly smacked her bottom. I hope you will chastise her.'

Joe-Ben was not sure he could fulfil Debbie's hopes. He was not in favour of smacking little girls' bottoms, or, indeed, any bottoms. He could only promise that he would speak seriously to his daughter, though he postponed carrying out this duty from holiday to holiday, and then forgot all about it.

Now she was returning to become a permanent member of the household, and for a short time the prospect troubled him. What on earth would he do with the child? Would she expect him to spend a great deal of time with her? Would she interfere with his work, expect to tramp the fields and woodlands with him, asking silly questions?

During each holiday he had considered it his duty to take Daisy on at least one expedition. Somehow these almost always proved to be disastrous, as when they visited London Zoo and she half choked a number of animals with sticky toffee, then ate an inordinate number of cream buns and was sick on the train.

Joe-Ben shuddered at such memories, but comforted himself with the recollection that she was seventeen, a young lady. No doubt she would have means of entertaining herself, and his mother could certainly make use of her around the house and the farm.

A week before Daisy was expected, Alice received a letter from her, which she took to Joe-Ben.

'What do you think, son? Daisy has written to me.' She sounded pleased, for it was the first time it had happened. During terms Daisy restricted herself to the obligatory weekly parental letter.

'That's nice,' Joe-Ben said, absently.

'She wants to bring a little friend with her.'

Joe-Ben was startled into paying attention. 'A what?'

'A friend.'

'For how long?'

'She doesn't say. The whole of the holidays, I suppose.'

'You've forgotten, Mother. Daisy won't be going back to school.'

'Oh, well, perhaps the friend will.'

'It will give you a great deal of work.'

Alice smiled. Her family, for as long as she could remember, had insisted she should not work so hard, but as they did not provide a remedy, she simply continued to do so.

'I don't mind. It's for you to decide. Do you wish me to refuse?'

Joe-Ben hesitated. The idea of two girls for weeks on end was not attractive. They would disrupt routine, expect different food at different times, complain of boredom. They would ask for unlimited hot water for frequent baths, would giggle, lounge around and probably smoke cigarettes. He wished he had been more strict with his daughter. Daisy was something of a problem, but Daisy twice over would be insufferable.

'I don't think — ' he began, then changed

his mind. 'Oh, all right. If you've no objection, let the friend come.'

He was out when they arrived, for he had forgotten they were coming. It was a radiant July day, and he left soon after sunrise, with pencils and drawing-pad and a packet of bread and cheese. Sussex possessed a wealth of butterflies, and July was the month of all others to find them. In the woodlands he came upon Fritillary and White Admiral, and saw the glorious Purple Emperor sailing over the oak trees. He stayed a while, watching and sketching, then continued to the open Downs, in search of the Chalk Hill Blue.

How many miles he covered that day he did not know, for he was not concerned with the figures of time and space, but when he reached Marlipins, by different and devious routes, shadows were long and the west was ablaze with colour.

He would have gone straight to his room, to put away his notes and drawings, but he heard the sound of unfamiliar voices, and remembered. He was ashamed of the sinking of his heart. It had been a wonderful day. He should not begrudge the necessity of playing the part of father and host. Always one had to descend from the heights to the mundane plains. At least, he thought, thankfully, his mother was entertaining the girls in the kitchen. A parlour conference would have been more than he could have borne.

At first he thought he had been mistaken. The lamp had not yet been lighted, and in the dusk the two ladies sitting there could not be the schoolgirls he had expected.

Then one of them stood up. 'Father.'

The change, he saw, was chiefly in her hair, which was piled high on top of her head. He had forgotten those two great moments in a girl's life, when the hair was put up and the skirts lengthened.

She went to him and kissed him on the cheek.

'Well, Daisy, you have quite grown up.' It sounded a fatuous remark to him, but what else could he say?

She beckoned to the other girl. 'This is my friend, Alix Petitjean.'

The girl held out a slim hand. 'How do you do, Monsieur — ' she hesitated ' — Elphick?'

'That is the name by which I am known. But you are French?'

'Yes.'

He found himself staring at her, for even in the dimness of the room she shone like a light. Her hair was dressed like Daisy's, but it was of that rare colour which could truly be described as golden. She was slim

161

and willowy, and tall enough for her eyes to be almost level with his.

'Alix,' he found himself asking, 'is that short for Alexandra?'

Daisy replied for her. 'No, it is not.' She spoke in a superior tone. 'It is Alix, after the wife of Henry the First, Alix la Belle.'

He could think of nothing more to say. It was Alice who took command. 'Now go and put your things away, JoeBen. It's time we had supper. Daisy, see if your Uncle Rose and Aunt Tirell are ready.'

There were no giggles from the two young ladies. Daisy conversed, chiefly with Tirell, in a refined and intelligent manner. Joe-Ben and Rose, both exceedingly hungry, gave their attention to the food, and Alix said nothing at all. Perhaps, Joe-Ben thought, she understood little English, or perhaps she was stupid. His mind was still full of those July butterflies. So beautiful they were that one could expect little from them except beauty.

7

The gay, who would be counted wise,
Think all delight in pastime lies;
Nor heed they what the wise condemn,
Whilst they pass time — Time passes them.
Godelin. 17th C.

At first there was a conspiracy of silence
to protect Benjy from any doubts as to his
eventual recovery. It was instigated by one of
the consultants, a man of advanced ideas.

'I have been in Vienna with Doctor Freud,'
he said, solemnly. 'We are discovering a great
deal about the mind, and it is my opinion
that it can influence the body more potently
than we realise. Your son must believe he
will walk again.'

Dolly wanted something more concrete.
'But will he?'

'You must instil the thought in his mind,
make him believe.'

'I'm not asking whether he will believe,'
Dolly persisted. 'I'm asking whether he will
walk.'

'Madam, I can promise nothing. It is a
matter of time.'

163

'Then what good will believing do?'

The doctor sighed. He wished women would not ask questions, especially questions he could not answer. Still, Dolly was no fool. She understood the importance of keeping Benjy's spirits up, and so she wore a smiling face when she was with him.

It was some time before Benjy showed any impatience. He was content to lie quietly because any movement was agony. He even derived a secret comfort from the realisation that it would be long before he could be expected to ride a horse again. His only fear was that Christopher might blame him for the accident.

'It wasn't my fault,' he said, pitifully. 'I did try to stay on.'

Christopher nodded. 'You've not had enough experience, but you'll learn.'

Benjy had a stab of terror. 'D'you mean I'll have to — that is, shall I ride Corporal Violet again?'

'Why not?' Christopher asked, cheerfully. 'Cruttenden is an excellent trainer. He's already mastered the horse. By the time you're ready the beast will be as meek as a lamb.'

Dolly was furious. 'What have you been saying to Benjy?' she demanded of Christopher.

'Nothing in particular. Why?'

'I've just found him in a dreadful state. Did you tell him he'd have to get up on that monster once more?'

'No. I only explained that Cruttenden is doing wonders for the animal.'

'Oh, yes!' Dolly exclaimed, scornfully. 'And do you suppose that will help Benjy's recovery?'

'It shouldn't make any difference.'

'That's all you know. He'd rather die than ride the creature.'

'Well, he can always refuse.'

'But he won't. Are you so blind that you can't see he'd do anything to please you? You're his hero.' She stared at her husband and added, bitterly, 'God knows why.'

She tried to reassure the boy. 'You'll never get on the horse again, or on any horse, for that matter. I'll see to it.' But it was useless. He looked at her almost with compassion, in no way deceived by her promises. He knew that Christopher was disappointed in him, and the knowledge hurt even more than his injured back.

It was not until Tom returned that Benjy showed any interest in life. Tom did not indulge in lamentation or treat Benjy like an invalid. He was too practical for that. 'You can't lie there for ever,' he said. 'You need fresh air.'

Benjy was stung into making a vigorous retort. 'Expect me to jump out of bed and turn somersaults?'

'No, but I could push you around if you had a wheel-chair.'

'I wouldn't be seen dead in one,' Benjy declared.

Tom laughed. 'You won't have to. They don't bury people in wheel-chairs.'

Such a remark would once have been the signal for a scuffle. Benjy would have leapt on Tom and they would have rolled and tussled like puppies. Now he felt tears of weakness coming into his eyes, and turned his head away.

All the same, Tom acted like a tonic. Benjy expressed a desire to get up, and Christopher sent for the doctors who, after protracted consultation, encased Benjy in plaster from neck to thighs, with the hope that after a month or two it might be possible to dispense with this and substitute a specially constructed surgical corset.

In the beginning Benjy was terrified. He feared sudden jolts; he feared the slightest slope might cause the chair to run away, or a stone beneath the wheel might overturn it. The outside world seemed strange and vast, an amble down the garden drive as dangerous as an expedition to the North Pole.

166

Only in Tom had he any confidence, and he would allow no one else to push his chair.

'I can manage it easily,' Dolly assured him. 'It runs so smoothly.'

He would not listen. 'You're only a woman. You couldn't hold it back on a hill.'

'But you can't expect Tom to be with you every moment of the day,' his mother told him. 'He has his own life to live.'

As soon as she had said it she realised her mistake, for the stricken expression on Benjy's face made her heart ache for him.

Tom had been home for a week when Christopher said to him, 'We'll go to the races tomorrow.'

Tom looked surprised. 'You haven't a horse running, have you?'

'No, but that doesn't matter. Owners have to move around, meet people, see what's going on.'

'Thank you, Father, but I don't think I'll come.'

'Not come? Don't talk rubbish! You have to get to know the ropes, same as I have.'

'I can't leave Benjy.'

'What!' exploded Christopher. 'Never heard such a lame excuse in my life. His mother can look after him, and if that's beyond her, haven't I a house full of servants? You don't

167

have to be nursemaid to a cripple.'

Tom's eyes narrowed. 'Don't ever let Benjy hear you call him that.'

'Well, it's what he is, isn't it?'

'And who made him what he is?'

'Now, then, Tom, don't get shirty with me!' Christopher coaxed. 'I don't always put things as polite as I might. I'm sorry for Benjy, of course, but I've got to think of you. If we're to make a success of this racing business we've got our work cut out. There's men who've been in it for a lifetime, men wealthier than I am. It's a tough job, full of tricks and hanky-panky, as you'll find out.'

'No, Father, I shan't find out, because I don't want to go in for it.'

Christopher stared at him, incredulous. 'You said you did.'

'No. You just took it for granted that I would.'

'Well, you'll have to do *something*, now you've left school. How d'you think you'll pass the time?'

That was how Christopher *would* put it, Tom thought, grimly. How to pass the time. Not how to earn a living, how to keep yourself and your family from starving, which was the problem of the greater part of the population. No, for Christopher and other so-called gentlemen time was the problem, a gap to be filled by some kind of occupation, honourable or otherwise.

'Time will pass well enough,' Tom said. 'I shall earn my living.'

'That's not necessary. You'll be provided for.'

'I'm not interested in your money.'

Christopher winced. Only Tom could hurt him. No other living person had that power. 'One day my money will be yours. You've a right to it. I'm your father.'

'What about Benjy? He's the one who needs it.'

'Never mind Benjy.' Christopher dismissed him with a gesture. 'What of you? How could you earn your living? Have you learnt anything useful at that posh school?'

'I think I have. What I want to be is an electrical engineer.'

Christopher blinked. 'What?'

'It's coming, Father. It's growing. It's the profession of the future.'

Calm, stolid Tom was glowing with enthusiasm, and Christopher felt a stab of jealousy. 'You want to be a navvy?' he sneered.

'No. I had a master who told me that there are now four learned professions — the Church, Law, Medicine and Engineering. I've had a good general education, so that's a start, but it's a long and special training, to become a consulting electrician. There would have to be a premium paid.' Tom paused and then looked up hopefully. 'You wouldn't object to giving me that, would you?'

'I certainly would,' Christopher replied, promptly. 'I've spent thousands of pounds getting this racing stable started, and I'll require thousands more. If you think I'm going to waste money on every hare-brained scheme — '

'It's not hare-brained,' Tom insisted. 'One of these days you'll have this house blazing with electric light. In London and other big towns they're installing it more and more. They used to call it the luxury of the rich, but now — '

'Spare me the lecture! I'm not interested. If I am paying to have you trained it will have to be for something worthwhile. Now, are you coming to the races?'

The light went out of Tom's face. He looked sullen. 'No, I'm not,' he said, shortly, and turned and walked away.

Christopher was exceedingly angry. He wondered, with self-pity, what he had done to deserve two such unsatisfactory sons, one a funk, the other a pig-headed fool. Hadn't he done everything for them, given them the best?

He went alone to the races and, because he was bored, decided to place a few bets. It was the first time he had done so, for he was scarcely more than a child when his father made him swear he would never gamble.

'You know how it was with your grandfather. It's a disease, boy. He could never resist betting on a horse or a pack of playing-cards. That's why he had to sell Marlipins, our family home, and bring me out here.'

'Don't you like Australia?' young Christopher had asked.

His father's eyes took on a dreamy look. Thomas Waldron was remembering his boyhood in that country which with the passing of time had come to take on some of the qualities of a paradise. Whenever they were plagued by drought he would think of the soft English rain. Were any other fields ever so green?

'Yes, Australia's fine,' he replied. 'It's made money for us, brought back what your grandfather threw away, that and more. Maybe one day you'll go home to England, but you swear to me, here and now, that you'll not follow in your grandfather's footsteps.'

Naturally young Christopher swore, and was proud to do so. It had not occurred to him to break his promise, and he did not intend to do so now. He was a level-headed man, he assured himself, and the risking of a few pounds certainly would not brand a man a gambler.

He found people friendly, especially after he told them he was establishing a stable and owned several horses. They were only too willing to give him tips, and their confidence reinforced his own. After all, there was only one way to make racing pay. One had to be in the know, mix with other owners, with trainers, with jockeys. It was the poor ignorant public which furnished the wherewithal for book-makers to live.

The fact that all the tipped horses lost on that day did not discourage him. His new friends explained the reasons why the animals had disappointed. It was all quite logical, and things would be better tomorrow.

He was in excellent spirits when he returned home. Say what you like, he thought, placing a bet on a horse added considerably to the excitement, and the expending of a hundred pounds or so for that excitement was neither here nor there.

When he reached the house he was told that none of the family was indoors. Master Tom had taken Master Benjy out in his chair. The mistress? No, they did not know where she was.

Christopher did not bother to go and look for her, which was probably just as well, Dolly happening to be in the rose garden with Peter Baker.

8

Daughter thou art old enough
to be a wedded wife.
                    '*Simon and Susan.*' *Anon.*

Of Farncombes — the new Farncombes
— there was only one part in which
Dolly found pleasure. She declared that
she detested the house, though sometimes
she felt 'detested' to be too strong a word. It
was spacious, warm and comfortable, if that
were only what one wanted from a house,
but she never came to feel it belonged to
her. It could have been an hotel in which
she was a passing guest.

The garden was a different matter. At
Marlipins she and Debbie had as children
been given penny packets of seed to sow
— marigold and candytuft and larkspur.

' 'Twill brighten an odd corner,' their
mother told them. She knew, as most farmers
did, that there was neither time nor space for
the growing of useless flowers.

It had been almost the same at the Queen
Anne house in the village, a noble residence
confined between adjacent properties and

possessing a diminutive parcel of land.

The grounds of Farncombes never ceased to fill Dolly with wonder. There was something almost sinful, she felt, about devoting so large an area to plants which could not be eaten either by man or beast, to fountains whose water served no useful purpose, to plantations of trees that produced fruit only for their own reproduction.

Yet despite their lack of utility Dolly appreciated the beauty of those decorative acres. They soothed her restless spirit, and she spent hours wandering through the various gardens, watching the change in growth and season, sometimes talking to one of the gardeners, marvelling at the knowledge required to grow those things she had looked upon as unprofitable luxuries.

On the day Christopher went alone to the races she had expected to have Benjy in her care, but by the time she was ready she found Tom had already taken him out. She was disappointed, but as she could think of nothing in the house to occupy her she made her way to the rose garden where the carefully tended beds were a blaze of colour.

She wished there were something she could do with roses. She could pick them for the house, of course, but arranging flowers

175

seemed to her to be a waste of time, and so she left it to one of the servants.

Christopher called her lazy. 'A lady should do the flowers herself.'

'Why?'

'I don't know. It's the proper thing, that's all.'

'I don't want to do the proper thing.'

'We know that, don't we?' he sneered.

Dolly sighed. Why had she come back to Christopher? Why hadn't she kept to her first intention, to bring Benjy up by herself? If she had done so, he wouldn't now be in a wheel-chair. Sometimes, since the accident, she had felt that she actually hated Christopher.

It was then that she saw a man coming towards her, walking briskly along one of the paths, bold as brass.

She was angry at the intrusion and, as soon as he was close enough to hear her, she said, 'The tradesman's entrance is at the back.'

'I'm not a tradesman.'

His clothes were shabby and dusty, as though he had walked far, and there was something insolent in his tone. For a moment she was afraid, and glanced round to see whether one of the gardeners was near, but there was no one in sight and the gardens were so quiet that the buzz of a bee working on a rose filled the air.

'Well, what do you want?'

'To see you.'

She looked more closely at him, then took a step forward. Wasn't there something familiar? 'Peter?'

'You've taken a time recognising me,' he said, with some bitterness.

'Good gracious, what did you expect? How long is it? Seventeen years? Eighteen?'

'About that.'

'You've changed.'

'So have you.'

She gave a little laugh, chiefly to hide her embarrassment. 'That's not very gallant.'

'Nor were you. Why should it be an insult to tell a woman she has changed, whereas a man — '

'Where have you been?'

'Everywhere. You know me. I never stay long.'

'But you've come back here.'

'Yes. I had a fancy to see my child, son or daughter. Which is it?'

'You didn't fancy staying to see him born,' Dolly retorted. 'You just couldn't get away fast enough.'

'So it's a boy. Good!'

Dolly studied him. He was thinner, almost haggard, and he had the appearance of a man who had lived rough. 'You should go away before Christopher returns. I don't think he'd welcome you.'

'Does he believe the boy is mine?'

'Sometimes. Other times he seems to persuade himself that Benjy is his.'

'What do you believe?'

She shrugged her shoulders. 'I've stopped asking myself the question.'

'Well, can I see my son?'

'See him? No, I don't think so.'

'Why not? We needn't tell him who I am.'

She hesitated. 'You wouldn't like it. He's in a wheel-chair.'

His face expressed horror. 'You mean he wasn't born right? He's a cripple?'

'No. He's a fine boy. I mean, he was — ' Tears filled her eyes. 'He was thrown from a horse.'

'But he'll get better?'

Dolly shook her head, not in denial but in doubt. 'We don't know. It was about four months ago.'

'Poor kid! You've not had much luck, have you, Dolly, what with one thing and another? You've still got Christopher, though, Christopher and his money.'

'And a lot of good it has done me!' she burst out. Misery flooded her, and nostalgia for that brief time when Peter had loved her, or had seemed to love her. 'I think,' she said, slowly, 'that on the whole Debbie has been the lucky one.'

Had Debbie heard, she would not have agreed at that moment, for she was having a confidential and unpleasant talk with Faith.

'You cannot tell me you have been over-eating,' Debbie declared. 'In fact, I've noticed you are eating less than usual.'

'Maybe it's because I'm constipated,' Faith said, sullenly.

'Well, whatever it is I shall ask Tirell to examine you.'

'Oh, no! Don't do that! Please, Mother, don't!' Faith spoke quickly and urgently, and Debbie's eyes narrowed.

'What is the matter with you, child? What is worrying you? Are you in any kind of trouble?'

As soon as she spoke, Debbie wished she had not used that word. Trouble. Trouble was a euphemism for a specific disaster. Surely it was not possible Faith could be guilty of such wickedness.

Faith realised she must answer the questions with which she was being bombarded. There was no way out. Her mother was waiting.

'All right.' Her voice came in a croak and she cleared her throat. 'All right. I'm going to have a baby.'

Spoken aloud the words sounded terrible. It was as if they had not really been true until she heard herself saying them.

Her mother became so deathly pale that Faith thought she would faint; but then the blood came back in a rush. Her face reddened, and even her eyes were fiery. 'You fool! You stupid little fool!'

Faith backed away. She was afraid her mother would attack her physically. 'I didn't mean it,' she muttered helplessly.

'Didn't mean it? Don't tell me you didn't know what you were doing. I brought you up decently, and this is how you repay me, you filthy slut! When did it happen?'

'At Cuckoo Fair.'

Debbie was thunderstruck. 'God help us! In your own village! In broad daylight!'

'No, it was at night.'

'But you were home before dark.'

Faith hung her head. 'We went out again.'

'That Beatrice Luff. I suppose she led you astray. No wonder she doesn't dare to show her face here again. Oh, yes, my girl, I've had a letter from her mother, stating that Beatrice won't be returning to school. I suppose she is in the same condition.'

'I don't think so. She didn't say.'

'No. She had more sense. You were the one to get caught.' Then, thinking this

180

sounded as though she sanctioned the act while condemning the result, she added, 'Fornication is a deadly sin.'

It required a great effort for Debbie to ask the next question. 'Do you know the man?'

For a moment Faith did not understand. 'The man? Oh! You mean the boy who — it was Caleb Stower.'

Debbie's mouth distorted as though she sucked a lemon. 'Farmer Stower's son. Really, Faith, you might have chosen some-one more — I'll go over to Stower's at once. The sooner the matter is settled, the better.'

'You mustn't!' Faith exclaimed, in alarm. 'His father will be angry.'

'I should hope so,' Debbie replied, crisply. 'If he is half as angry as I am, he will be very angry indeed. They are respectable people, in their way.'

'But you can't do anything,' Faith said, wearily, 'it's too late.'

'I certainly intend to do something.'

'Well, what?'

'I shall insist he marries you, of course.'

Faith stared at her mother in horror. 'Marry? Marry Caleb? I would rather die.'

'I don't believe you would. In any case there is no alternative. I have no desire for illegitimate grandchildren.'

Faith burst into tears. 'Oh, no, Mother! Please, Mother! I couldn't do it. I don't like him.'

'You liked him well enough to be intimate with him,' Debbie reminded her, grimly.

'I didn't. He made me.'

Debbie sighed. 'If you accused him of rape you would have to prove it, and that would cause a great scandal.' Rape, she thought, she knew all about that, and her heart softened. She wanted to hold the girl in her arms and comfort her. Perhaps after all Faith had been taken by force, but it would be her word against the boy's, and the publicity would be merciless. She steeled herself against her compassion.

'Court cases involving sex are very nasty,' she said. 'A thing like that would ruin the school.'

Faith sniffed and then blew her nose. 'Your precious school isn't much of a success.'

'It brings us a living, of a kind. Besides, we have to think of the family. Joe-Ben is becoming famous, and Rose is doing well. Then there's Tirell. A doctor must be respected. My grandfather was always respected, and so was my mother, and still is. Even when things went wrong, they protected the family.'

Faith lost her temper. 'I don't hold with

it,' she raged. 'Why should I marry a man I don't love, just for the sake of the family? It will ruin my whole life.'

'It may do,' Debbie agreed, sombrely, 'because that is what you are, a ruined woman.'

There was nothing Faith could do to prevent her mother visiting the Stowers. Debbie put on her best clothes and went forth valiantly like a charger into battle, while Faith waited in trepidation, hoping that Caleb would refuse, and that his father would not be coerced.

She gazed into her mother's face when she returned, searching for news, but her expression revealed nothing. Debbie went upstairs and changed back into her workaday clothes.

When she came down, Faith could bear it no longer. 'For goodness sake tell me what happened?'

Debbie raised her eyebrows. 'At Stowers? They have invited you to dinner next Sunday.' She paused, then added, 'You had better be pleasant to them.'

9

Ten-button Gloves.

Sunday morning was church-going, which no member of the Marlipins household dared avoid. Joe-Ben might think of flowery meadows and sun-dappled woods; Rose might make a mental list of urgent work awaiting; but still they walked circumspectly up the path between the tombs into the cool church. Even Tirell had only once missed the ceremony, and that was because she was needed at an imminent birth.

Alice it was who had maintained the importance of family worship. Shining with soap and water, dressed in their best clothes, they congregated and set out together, a small company of Christian soldiers.

Visitors were expected to conform, and so there was something like consternation when on the first Sunday after their homecoming Daisy arrived downstairs without Alix.

Alice sighed. 'We shall be late.' Then she remembered something. 'Oh, dear! Is she Roman?'

'She is Catholic of course.' Daisy reproved

184

her grandmother, 'but she has no objection to attending our village church. No, the trouble is her ten-button gloves.'

'Ten-button what?' Alice asked, bewildered.

'Gloves. They take a long time to fasten. They have extremely tiny pearl buttons. I did offer to help her, but she preferred to do them herself. She has lost her button-hook.'

'Well, I don't know what the Vicar will say, I'm sure, disrupting his service for a pair of — '

Alix came into the room. It was, Joe-Ben thought, like placing an amaryllis in a bunch of horse-daisies. He wanted to express his disapproval, but her apologetic expression was disarming. 'Do you wait for me?' she asked. 'I am very sorry.'

'We do wait for you,' Alice told her, grimly, 'and we'll be lamentable late if we don't walk smartish. And while you're here there's no need to doll yourself up. I tell Daisy to wear her country clothes.'

Without intention Joe-Ben found himself saying, 'I think Alix looks elegant. It's good for joskins like us to see a fine lady occasionally.'

His mother glanced at him in surprise, but said no more, and led the way, as she always did by virtue of her seniority, now that she was a widow. Rose followed with Tirell, then

Debbie with Constance and Faith, and last went Joe-Ben with Daisy on one side of him and Alix on the other.

Alice set the pace, trying to hurry without losing the dignified gait proper to the occasion. Rose nudged Tirell. 'We are a cross between a wedding and a funeral,' he whispered, and she laughed, drawing from Alice a backward glance of censure.

'Why does Grandmother take all this so seriously?' Faith asked. 'What does it matter if we're late? We know the service by heart anyway. I'm getting out of breath. I shouldn't hurry, in my condition.'

'I've told you not to mention your condition,' Debbie hissed, 'not until you're married, and not then in public.'

'It's a waste of time,' Constance said, with a superior air. 'People can count, you know. Up to nine anyhow.' She was feeling extremely virtuous because of Faith's downfall, and for the first time was conscious of her virginity as an asset. 'Catch me letting any man mess about with me!'

'Don't talk like that!' Debbie scolded. 'It sounds so vulgar.'

Alix, who had not heard the snatches of conversation, was looking wistfully at the little group in front of her. 'How happy to have a family so large.'

'Why? Have you no brothers and sisters?' Joe-Ben asked.

'I have no one. I am an orphan.'

'Her father was a sea-captain,' Daisy explained. 'He was drowned in a shipwreck, and her mother died of a broken heart.'

'I am sorry.'

'Oh, you need not be,' Daisy told him. 'It was a long time ago. You don't remember them, do you, Alix?'

Alix shook her head. 'But still I miss them.'

Daisy shrugged her shoulders. 'You can't miss what you haven't had. I never had a mother.'

'Everyone has a mother.'

Joe-Ben wished they would talk of something else, and for once he was glad when the church came into sight.

After the service a number of people lingered, exchanging greetings and news with acquaintances, and Joe-Ben, not feeling in the mood for company, strolled away through the churchyard towards Joan's grave.

To his surprise the two girls were there, and for some reason this pained and annoyed him. 'Are you being shown the sights of Brambleden?' he inquired of Alix sarcastically.

She replied seriously. 'No. Daisy wishes

me to see where her mother is buried. It is all she has of her.'

'I'm sorry,' Joe-Ben apologised, ashamed. 'I suppose I've come to think of this as my private property. It isn't, of course.'

'She was young,' Alix said. 'Not much more than a year older than I.'

'Then you must be — '

'Eighteen and a half.'

'And still at school.'

'No. I leave now, as Daisy does.'

'Alix is going to be an artist,' Daisy said, importantly.

He felt a prick of irritation, and did not recognise it as jealousy. 'Thousands of young women imagine they can draw and paint. Studying in Paris, or in Timbuctoo, won't give you talent if you don't possess it.'

'Did you not study?'

Joe-Ben laughed. 'I had to work for a living, copying legal documents all day until my hand was almost too tired to hold the pen, then walking six-and-a-half miles home. No, I had no time for study.'

'Yet you are successful.'

'Perhaps.' Suddenly he caught at her hand and lifted it. 'Take off those things!'

'Pardon?'

'Those gloves.'

'But — '

'How do you imagine you can be an artist if you confine your hands in strait-jackets? Come on! Give them air! Let them breathe! Here! I'll help you.'

He turned her hand over, exposing the buttons which were so tiny that even his artistic fingers felt clumsy. He pulled harder, and one button flew off.

'That's done it!' Daisy exclaimed. 'You'll never find it here.'

Here? He became aware of where they were, and it appeared to him that he had been guilty of unseemly behaviour. He dropped her hand and without another word turned and walked away.

That afternoon Daisy said 'Alix would like you to show her some of your work.'

Joe-Ben felt again the touch of resentment which he was beginning to associate with Daisy or Alix or both of them. 'Have you made yourself Alix's spokeswoman?' he asked, coldly. 'Or is she afraid to ask for herself?' Both girls were silent, and he had to prompt them. 'Well?'

Daisy got up and flounced out of the room. Joe-Ben looked at Alix in exasperation. 'What is the matter with her?'

'She is angry,' Alix replied, solemnly, 'and I do not fear to speak for myself. Please may I be permitted to see your work?'

'Certainly. You may borrow my books.'

Alix smiled. 'Oh, not your books. Those I have read. Daisy has them all.'

Joe-Ben stared. 'Daisy? I don't remember giving her — '

'No. You do not give. She buys from the bookshop close to our school. Each one she orders when it is published.'

'I didn't think she was interested.'

'What girl is not proud, who has a famous father?'

'I see.' For some reason he was disappointed. So Daisy's motive for buying his books was that she might boast to her schoolfellows.

'If I could look at your pictures, the original drawings and paintings — '

'Why not?' He took her to his study, laid out a selection of his illustrations, and waited for what he expected would be the usual schoolgirl gush.

When it did not come he was somewhat nettled. 'Don't you like them?'

She laughed. 'Were I to praise you it would be — what do you call it? Une impudence?'

'A cheek?'

'Yes. We know they are very good, do we not?'

'I didn't ask whether you considered them good. I asked if you liked them.'

'Would it be a — a cheek to want to see your note-books, the sketches you make when you are in the open air?'

From a drawer he took a sheaf of papers and slid them in front of her. 'There! I have hundreds more.'

'Ah!' She drew a deep breath. 'These I like.'

'They are rough.'

'They are alive. Here you have nature around you. You draw as you see.'

Suddenly his irritation vanished. He reached for a notebook. 'These are my latest. Butterflies.'

'Oh, yes. Some I know. There is the fritillaire.'

'That is the High Brown Fritillary, and next to it the Silver-washed. I am planning a small book about small, coloured things, which so often we miss. Butterflies, moths, dragon-flies, beetles as bright as emeralds — '

'It will be beautiful.'

He was aware of a sense of uneasiness. 'Alix, I don't think I've been very hospitable. I've probably sounded rude, a grumpy old bear — '

'Monsieur — Mister Elphick, I do assure you — '

'Don't call me that!' he snapped. 'I am Joe-Ben.'

'Joe-Ben, I do not blame you. I am sorry for you. You are an unhappy man.'

He stared at her in astonishment. 'Unhappy? I am fortunate. I can do the work I like. I make sufficient money for all I need. Most people would envy me.'

'It is a pity you cannot love Daisy. She too is unhappy. She admires you so much.'

'Daisy?' He spoke sharply. 'She has had every advantage, but she is becoming a spoilt and frivolous young woman.'

'It is Daisy who makes you angry, because she is not her mother.'

With an effort Joe-Ben controlled himself. 'Now, Alix, you should not interfere in matters which do not concern you.'

Relentlessly she continued. 'Do you think often of your wife?'

'As little as possible.'

'But you loved her?'

'Yes, but thinking of the past only brings sorrow. When I remember my loss I am unhappy, and when I remember our time together I am equally unhappy, because I know it can never come again.'

'Yet you tell me you are not an unhappy man,' Alix reminded him, bewildered.

'That is true, and it's the reason why I don't allow myself to think of Joan.'

'I don't understand you, Joe-Ben.'

'I wouldn't expect you to. How could a beautiful young girl understand a tetchy old widower?'

He spoke lightly, ignoring his sensitive finger-tips which tingled with the longing to stroke that shining golden head.

10

Truth is the shattered mirror strown
In myriad bits.

Sir Richard Burton.

Dolly had no intention of resuming any kind of relationship with Peter Baker, but she ran into him by chance one day in the village.

'You still here?'

He grinned. 'Funny how often people ask that. Reckon I've a talent for being unwanted.'

'I'm not surprised,' Dolly retorted, 'if you behave like you did when you worked for Christopher.'

'Oh, I don't seduce all the wives. Most of 'em aren't as pretty as you.'

It was his usual easy way of talking. Dolly told herself it did not mean anything, but all the same she was pleased. 'How long are you staying?'

He shrugged. 'Depends. There's plenty of country work at present, with fruit-picking, and harvest coming along.'

'So you're still a — ' She hesitated.

'Failure' was the word that came into her mind.

'Rolling stone? I don't know. Maybe I've rolled to the bottom of the hill by now.' He looked sideways at her and dropped his bantering tone. 'I don't want to leave until I've seen my son.'

'Well — ' She was undecided. It would be foolish to court trouble, but she lived in a state of chronic boredom, and despite the passing years Peter held his appeal for her. 'If you were very discreet — You must on no account let Benjy know you have any connection with him or with me.'

'Oh, come now, Dolly! D'you think I'm likely to go up to him and say, 'Hello, son! I'm your daddy'?'

'You must have another name, in case the boys mention your visit to Christopher. You see, Tom will be there as well.'

'Who the hell is Tom?'

'Debbie's youngest. We adopted him.'

'My! Christopher is a rare one for collecting other people's children. When can I see Benjy?'

'Come to luncheon one day. You can say you know Joe-Ben and Rose, that you were friends years ago.'

'Right! And I'll call myself — let's see — Yes, Clayton Slyfield.'

195

Dolly stared at him, wide-eyed. 'Gracious! Why choose a name like that?'

'Because it sounds authentic. Who would want to invent such a name? Tell me, when will Christopher be away from home?'

'Every day,' Dolly replied, promptly. 'That is, every day when there is racing. If it's in Scotland or the north of England he stays overnight. He is a great traveller on the railway.'

'I've heard talk in the village of his horses. How does he manage his stable, if he's away most of the time?'

'He leaves it to his trainer, Mr Cruttenden.' Dolly paused, then added, 'Christopher seems to have become interested in betting.'

'Lucky to be able to afford it,' Peter said, drily. He found himself pitying Dolly. Poor kid, she'd made a big mistake when she married Christopher Waldron, and it looked as if she'd not yet finished paying for it.

Dolly smiled ruefully. 'Maybe he can afford it, but he doesn't like losing. As soon as he arrives home I can tell whether he's had a good day or a bad one. It's in his face and his voice, even in the way he walks.'

For several days before Peter's visit she regretted having extended the invitation, and she was on tenterhooks from the moment he entered Farncombes. He had never been notable for tact. What if he should forget his assumed name, or drop some hint concerning his past association with Benjy's mother?

But she had to admit to herself that Peter behaved with admirable discretion, and when the boys had gone she said as much. 'Thank you, Peter! I was nervous, but I need not have worried. You were most tactful.'

Peter scowled. 'I could kill that bastard.'

'Christopher?' But there was no need to question whom he meant.

'To ruin a fine boy like that! Will he always be crippled?'

'Christopher consulted the most eminent doctors, but they seem unable to tell us anything definite. He may walk again one day, but I believe he'll never be strong or athletic. Christopher wanted to make a jockey of him.'

'Christopher wanted!' Peter mocked. 'Whatever Christopher wants seems to end in disaster. Are you resigned to staying with him for the rest of your life, Dolly?'

She lifted her hands and then dropped them. 'What else can I do?'

'Still unable to abandon the flesh-pots, eh?'

'It's not only myself,' she insisted. 'It's Benjy. He needs servants, care and attention.'

'Things which his mother is too lazy to provide,' Peter said, savagely.

'That's not fair. There's Tom to be considered, too. The boys are devoted to one another. If I left Christopher I'd have to take Tom as well, and I don't believe Christopher would ever allow it. He thinks the world of Tom.'

'More than of Benjy? Why? The boy is no relation of his.'

'I don't understand it,' Dolly confessed. 'It has always been a mystery to me. You see how difficult it is.'

Peter nodded, and did not pursue the subject. Instead he asked, abruptly, 'May I come again?'

'I'm not sure that you should. The servants might say something to Christopher to make him suspicious.'

'So you are content never to see me.'

She answered quickly, 'No!' then wondered if it were true. Surely he could not matter to her, after all this time. He had been hard, selfish, inconstant, and had finally left her. What could he want from her now, except Christopher's money?

The boys also wondered what he wanted, but vaguely, without any particular interest. 'Not a bad chap,' was Benjy's verdict, and then he asked, with more enthusiasm, 'Where shall we go this afternoon?'

It was some six weeks since Tom had finally left school, and he had given considerable thought to Marlipins and its residents, so close, yet so isolated from them. For as long as he could remember, the farm had been out of bounds. This Christopher had stated categorically, and only once since the fire had Tom broken the rule. But now that they were older it did seem ridiculous that the land right next to them should be forbidden territory.

'He treats us like children,' Tom said.

'Who does?'

'Father.'

Automatically Benjy sprang to Christopher's defence. 'Nothing strange in that. Parents don't believe we grow up.'

'Then we must make them believe. Tell you where we're going. To Marlipins.'

Benjy turned his head and stared at him. 'Tom, we can't!'

Tom began to walk briskly, pushing the chair. 'We'll go across the fields, past the Hammer Pond.'

'Father's had all the hedges wired.'

'I know a place where we can get under.'

Benjy was afraid. Even now he did not have complete confidence in his wheel-chair or in those who propelled it. To go across the fields meant gates and ditches, nettles and brambles. 'We'll get into trouble,' he said, doubtfully. 'There's a feud or something between our families.'

'Not on their side. I went there once, after the fire, and Mrs Aylwin talked to me. Really she's our Aunt Debbie, and she was very nice.'

'You went there? You didn't tell me.'

'I didn't tell anybody.'

'But we never had secrets from each other.'

There was a lump in Benjy's throat. He wanted to cry, and at the same time he wished desperately he were well and whole again, so that he could punch Tom hard, make his nose bleed, give him a black eye.

Tom wanted to explain, without hurting Benjy, but he was not sure how to do it. 'It's different when you're kids. After you grow up there are things you don't tell.'

'There shouldn't be,' Benjy grumbled. He felt sorry for himself. How could he have secrets, when there were always people around him, doing things for him?

Carefully Tom negotiated the chair under the barbed wire. The ditch was a more serious obstacle. Benjy gritted his teeth and clung to the arms of the chair to prevent himself being thrown out as the front wheels dipped down. It was almost worse finding himself lying horizontally as they climbed the other side.

'You're a rotter.'

'No, I'm not.'

'Yes, you are. I won't let you take me out again unless you keep to the road.'

'It's all right,' Tom assured him. 'We'll come back by the road if you like. You said it was dull, though, and you wanted adventure.'

'We shan't find adventure here,' Benjy said, sourly.

But they did find adventure of a kind, for as they passed the Hammer Pond they saw a girl walking by the water. It was Daisy, and she was in an extremely bad temper. It was not fair, she thought. She had invited Alix to stay at Marlipins to be a companion for her. And what had happened? Her father had purloined Alix to be a companion to him. Today they had departed shortly after breakfast for a long country ramble. Of course they had asked her to accompany them. For politeness' sake, she thought, miserably. But what would have been the use of that? Half of the time they would be talking of art, which did not interest Daisy in the least, and the other half of the time her father would be teaching Alix

201

things about birds and animals which Daisy had known since cradle days. So she had refused to join them. She hoped they would miss her, but she didn't really believe they would.

When she saw the two boys she felt a flicker of interest. There might be some entertainment here.

She strolled over to them. 'You're trespassing.'

To Tom she seemed very elegant and grown-up, but he put on a bold face, 'Is this your land?'

'Of course!' She used her most refined tone. 'Hammer Pond was part of one of the earliest iron works in Sussex. This lake turned the water-wheel, and my ancestors were iron-masters who made some of the cannon that destroyed the Spanish Armada.'

Tom was suitably impressed. 'What's your name?'

'I'm Daisy, and my father is Joe-Ben Elphick. He writes books and paints pictures, and he's famous.'

'I've heard of him,' Benjy admitted.

Daisy smiled. 'Naturally.'

'We didn't intend to trespass,' Tom apologised.

'Well, I suppose you have a right to be here,' Daisy allowed, 'considering we are related, but since our families are scarcely on speaking terms — I suppose you are my cousin Ninian.'

'No, I am Tom.'

She looked closely at him, and a mischievous imp suggested that considerable amusement could be derived from this meeting. She well knew she should disclose nothing of family affairs, probably was not credited with being aware of them, but she had overheard many conversations. She had been a quiet child, sitting silent in a corner, listening while the gossip flowed around her, the arguments, the bitterness and the anger.

'You were christened Ninian, after your father.'

Tom frowned. 'What are you talking about?'

'Haven't they told you that you were adopted?'

'It's not true. You are wrong.' He wanted to stop her, wanted to forget what she had said.

For a moment she was afraid, wondering whether she had gone too far, whether there would be repercussions, but then she reflected that at some time he would have to know the truth. 'I expect they were going to tell you when you were older,' she said, innocently.

His eyes narrowed. 'You're lying.'

'How dare you say such a thing! You can ask them. You can ask anyone. Your mother is Aunt Debbie. She was left a widow, and she was poor, because Uncle Ninian was only the village schoolmaster. You were her sixth child, and so she gave you to Aunt Dolly and Uncle Christopher. They wanted a companion for Benjy, a brother for him.'

Tom knew it was true. It had to be. No one would make up a story like that. He felt sick and betrayed, and a burning anger was building up in him. He wanted to do something terrible to this girl for what she had done to him, but beneath his rage a spark of reason insisted that she was not the one to blame. One should not take vengeance on a messenger. He had to face those who had wronged him.

He turned and ran, pushing the wheel-chair before him. Over the rough field he went, the wheels bumping and leaping, while Benjy shouted and screamed in terror.

11

For he that goes abroad, lays little up
in storing.

William Cleland.

Usually it was Tom who carried Benjy up the
stairs to his room. Christopher had engaged
a muscular young manservant for this and
other tasks requiring physical strength, but
Benjy preferred Tom. On the afternoon of
their encounter with Daisy, however, Benjy
would not allow Tom near him and pushed
him away.

'Don't touch me!' he shouted, almost
hysterical after their headlong sprint across
the fields. 'You tried to kill me.'

Tom was out of breath, still angry and
bewildered. 'Don't be silly! Why would I
want to do that?'

'Because you're not my brother. Because
you don't belong here any more.'

Tom turned away. He wanted to be
alone, to have time to think, and then he
wanted to confront Christopher, to demand
an explanation.

Christopher arrived home late and in a

205

bad mood. His betting losses that day had far exceeded those on any previous day. He had succumbed to the dangerous practice of doubling up and, though he was still convinced he would recover his losses, the strain on even his considerable fortune was beginning to worry him. Fellow-punters assured him it was merely a matter of courage and endurance. He believed them, and believed himself to possess those necessary qualities, but he had reached the stage when he preferred not to assess the current state of his finances.

Dolly said, 'Tom wants to see you.'

Christopher yawned. 'What about? I'm tired.'

'I don't know. They haven't told me anything, but both boys seem rather upset. I'll send Tom to you, and then I'm going to bed.'

Tom stood looking down at the man he had known as his father. He thought, 'Now I don't have to try to love you. I don't have to pretend,' and there was relief in the thought.

He said, 'Why have you deceived me? All these years you have lied to me.'

'What are you talking about?' Christopher asked.

'You are not my father.'

'And what has given you that cock-eyed notion?'

'It's no good. The secret's out. Everybody knows.' Tom paused, then added, with bitterness, 'Everybody except me.'

He was not sure what to expect. He knew Christopher to be a violent man, discounting the beatings he and Benjy had received, and of which they thought no more than of the traditional school canings. There had been the time when Christopher had knocked down an insolent servant, and twice Tom had seen him slap Dolly's face.

So he stiffened and waited. He was not afraid, but he was not going to submit to an assault. To his surprise Christopher took out a cigarette and lighted it. He was smiling.

'You have your facts wrong, young man. I am your father.'

'I was adopted.'

'Well, you might say that, in a way. Dolly is not your mother.'

'But — '

'I'm sorry you had to hear this through idle gossip, and I want you to keep it to yourself. We have to protect the ladies, you know. A woman who loses her reputation loses everything. Your mother is Debbie, Dolly's twin sister.'

'That's what I was told.'

'What's all the fuss about, then?'

'You mean you and Mrs Aylwin — Aunt Debbie — committed adultery?'

'That's the legal and biblical term,' Christopher agreed, drily.

'What would you call it?'

Christopher blew an almost perfect smoke ring and observed it approvingly. 'I would call it a peccadillo. Really, old chap, you mustn't get too goody-goody. Judge not — you know.'

'Does Mother — ' In confusion he floundered, unable to bring himself to say 'Aunt Dolly' as he felt he should. 'Does she know?'

Christopher shook his head. 'No. She thinks Debbie's husband, the schoolmaster, was your father. Debbie had you christened Ninian, and she never told Dolly her secret. Twins though they are, there are some things they can't share.'

'What shall I do?' Tom wanted to know.

'Do? Nothing.'

'But I should be at Marlipins, with my mother.'

'No!' Christopher sprang to his feet. 'Your place is here, with me. We have a racing stable, and you are to help me run it.'

'I'm not interested in racing.'

Christopher started to shout. 'Then you'd better learn to be. Isn't it bad enough that one son has let me down?'

'Benjy? What has Benjy done? Is it his fault that you put him on a savage horse and crippled him for life?'

'That's enough! You'll obey me or by God I'll — '

Christopher advanced threateningly, then stopped, nonplussed, as Tom did not give way.

'We're not children now,' Tom reminded him.

Christopher wavered, and turned away. It was true. Tom was a husky young man. No chance of putting him across his knee and administering the chastisement which once had been efficacious. Still, there must be something he could do. The idea of Tom deserting him, living at Marlipins, was unbearable. Suddenly Christopher hated the rambling pseudo-castle he had built, hated it from its castellated walls to its massive doors studded with imitation nails. He had wanted to put shabby old Marlipins to shame, but it was the dignified, ancient house that shamed him.

He did not utter a word as Tom asked politely, 'May I go now?' Tom took this for permission and left the room.

209

Benjy asked eagerly, 'Is it true? Were you adopted?'

Tom shook his head. 'No. He's my father. He said so.'

'But that girl — '

'She was making it up. Or maybe she was just mistaken. Mother and Aunt Debbie are almost exactly alike.'

It hurt to lie to Benjy, but Tom believed it was the best thing to do. He did not think pride would allow him to remain at Farncombes as the acknowledged son of his father's adulterous liaison. Yet how could he leave Benjy? Benjy depended on him for so many services no servant could or would render. He thought, I am my brother's keeper, and he did not know which feeling was the stronger — gratification that he was doing his best for Benjy, or bitterness at the humiliation of finding himself illegitimate, fruit of the passing fancy of a faithless wife who had been glad to dispose of her bastard.

Dolly sensed something was troubling him. 'What's wrong, Tom? You're very quiet lately.'

'Am I?'

'You give all your time to Benjy. Don't you think you should go out with boys like yourself? You're only young once, and you're not a nurse.'

'I'm all right.'

She could get no further response from him, and let the matter drop. Perhaps he really did like looking after Benjy. Certainly it was convenient for Dolly, being able to get away without attracting notice. She had not intended to make a habit of meeting Peter, of this she assured herself, but somehow it happened. He had been discreet enough to find lodgings in Heathfield, a few miles away and accessible by railway.

'You can easily come over to me,' he said, 'whereas if I show my face too often in Brambleden — you can guess the rest.'

'How long are you staying?' She spoke casually, ignoring the quickened beating of her heart.

He glanced sideways at her. 'Depends on you, doesn't it?'

'I don't see why.'

'You ought to. I'm still partial to you.'

'You were ready enough to leave me, before.'

'I hadn't any money.'

'Have you got more now?'

'No, less.'

She burst out laughing. 'Peter, you are impossible. How can you manage to pay for your lodging?'

'I thought you might lend me something.'

'Why should I?'

'To keep me here.'

'How do you know I want you to stay?'

'You give yourself away every time you look at me, every time I make love to you.'

It was true. She did not trust him, sometimes wished he had not returned, but she could not resist him. She was bored, lonely, starved of physical love, starved of tenderness.

'I can give you a little money, not much.'

'Isn't Christopher generous?'

'I don't know. He pays the bills, and I hardly ever ask him for anything. Why should I?' Her voice rose. She spoke passionately. 'What is there here for me to buy? Why should I have beautiful clothes? I don't go anywhere. I can't remember when Christopher last took me out.'

'Poor kid!'

'Not such a kid. I'm growing old.'

'You've improved with age.'

'Have I? No, you're flattering me.'

'Doesn't matter, so long as you like it. Dolly, have you thought of leaving Christopher?'

'Of course I have! Once I actually left him, as you know.'

'I mean recently. Does he still insist Benjy is his son?'

'Most of the time. But occasionally, when he loses his temper, he taunts me with saddling him with his bailiff's by-blow. Do you ever feel your ears burning, Peter? That's when he's talking about you. Oh, I don't know. It all seems like play-acting to me, as though Christopher himself doesn't know what is the truth.'

'I suppose he has told people Benjy is his son.'

'Oh, yes. He swears it. He almost seems to persuade himself that he's Tom's father too, which is ridiculous.'

'It's Benjy I'm concerned with. Has it occurred to you that if you left Christopher and took Benjy with you, you could claim a very liberal allowance?'

'Could I?'

'Definitely. You could take the matter to court, if necessary. Think of it! A wealthy man with a reputation for violence and cruelty, a man who caused his son to be crippled. You can't imagine the sympathy you would arouse.'

Dolly's eyes narrowed. 'What's in it for you, Peter?'

He laughed softly, put his arm round her and drew her close. 'What's in it for me? Why, a son, a good income for which I don't have to work, and — '

She pulled herself away. 'I might have known it,' she declared, angrily.

He reached out for her. 'Wait for the third benefit.'

'Well? What's that?'

'And a lovely loving woman.'

12

What is a first love worth except to prepare for a second? What does the second love bring? Only regret for the first.

John Hay.

In her struggle to re-establish the prosperity of her school Debbie was determined to miss nothing which might prove advantageous, and the idea of enlisting Daisy came as an inspiration.

'What do you propose to do, now that you have left school?' she asked her niece.

Daisy shrugged her shoulders. 'I haven't decided.'

'You don't wish to study art in Paris, with your friend?'

'Goodness, no!' Daisy laughed scornfully. 'I'm no good at it. Besides, one artist in the family is enough.'

'Your French is excellent.'

'It ought to be. At Madame de Valmore's it was the only language permissible. Alix and I talk mostly in French when we are alone.'

'Then there are other things you learnt — deportment, dancing, elocution — I am about to send out my new prospectus. Why should I not conduct my academy in the style of a continental finishing school?'

'I suppose you could,' Daisy allowed.

'Daisy — ' Debbie took the girl's arm — 'Daisy, will you join me?'

For a moment Daisy did not reply and then she asked, 'Are you suggesting you would employ me?'

Debbie understood. She thought, 'Poor child! Feeling herself unwanted. How could Joe-Ben have been so insensitive? Now the idea of this school has given her a feeling of importance.' Aloud, she said, 'Would you consider a six-months trial period, to see how you like it? After that, if you decide on it as a profession, we could form a partnership.'

Daisy was not accustomed to show emotion, but now a small glow warmed her. 'What about Constance?' she asked. 'And Faith?'

'You mean they might be jealous? Well, Faith will soon be occupied with her baby. I'm glad to say she is settling down contentedly with Caleb. He really is quite a nice boy. Constance? I'm sure she will realise you have qualifications she does not possess. I will have the prospectus prepared at once.'

They worked on it together, Debbie and Daisy, and Daisy no longer thought to ask Alix each morning what she would like to do.

Alix and Joe-Ben did not even notice that Daisy was busy, and they made no arrangements for meetings or excursions. It was as if they drifted together, mingling imperceptibly like stream and river. Alix made no mention of a date for leaving Marlipins, and Alice's hospitality was never bounded by time.

It was Joe-Ben eventually who became aware that the end of autumn must mean a change in their way of life.

'It will soon be too cold to spend all day out of doors.'

'How do you pass the winter?' she asked him.

'Oh, that is when I collect together my notes and my pictures and assemble them into some kind of order. If there were no dark days of winter I don't believe I should ever write a book. Nature is my temptress. She makes me lazy and wanton.'

Alix put her hand on his arm. 'I do not want to leave you.'

'You can come again, in the spring.'

'No. If I go I do not think I shall ever come again.'

217

Her voice sounded infinitely sad, and he glanced at her in surprise. 'Ever is a long time,' he said, lightly.

'Yes, it is.' She paused for a few minutes, drawing on all the courage she possessed, and then she said, 'I love you, Joe-Ben.'

He was dumb-founded, even shocked. How could he treat such a declaration? He did not intend to be clumsy or cruel, but he was at a loss for words. 'This is just a schoolgirl infatuation.'

She flinched as though he had struck her. 'I am sorry, I did not intend to embarrass you.'

'I am old enough to be your father.' Even as he uttered the banal phrase he saw what he had done to her, and was contrite. 'Alix, it's not like that. I'm not embarrassed. I'm overwhelmed. You have — you have honoured me, and I shall always remember it.'

'Remember?' she echoed, passionately. 'Have you not too much of remembering? Have you not too much of sorrow?'

'Sorrow is the penalty we pay for being human.'

'I want to bring you happiness.'

'You have done, Alix. These past weeks I've been happier than — oh, happier than for years.'

She took a deep breath, as if from relief. 'There! You see? So I must stay with you.'

He shook his head. 'It's not so simple as that. If you mean what I think you mean — ' He broke off with a laugh which had become rare for him ' — and somehow I don't think you are suggesting we should live in sin — '

'Certainly not!'

'Then I must point out that you are a beautiful girl, and the last thing I want is to bring you grief. Were we to marry, I should be gone while you were still a young woman. I couldn't bear to make a widow of you, Alix darling.'

'Do you care? Have you just a small love for me?'

'I haven't dared think of it,' he said, slowly. 'I only know that when I'm with you it's as if I've come home. It's like peace after pain.'

'What then can prevent us? We will not fear the future. It is the time we are together that matters.'

'Alix, that weather we had at the end of September and the beginning of October, when it was so warm and the sun was shining, do you know what they call it?'

She shook her head.

'Blackberry-summer,' he told her. 'It is

219

calm and beautiful, but it doesn't last long. Well, this is my blackberry-summer. I thank God for it, but I can't take advantage of it.'

Her eyes filled with tears. 'What an obstinate man you are!'

Something else struck him, forcefully. 'Haven't you thought of Daisy? I had forgotten her until now. That's how it's been ever since she was born. I'm a rotten father. I've neglected her. I've never given her the love she deserves. How can I deal her a further blow by presenting her with you as a step-mother?'

Alix was stricken. 'Oh, Joe-Ben! You have found the most cruel thing to say.'

'Perhaps. But it's true. You know it is.'

Tears overflowed, poured down her cheeks. 'I cannot bear to think of you growing old, lonely, having nothing.'

'I shall have the stars, and the indestructable grass, and the bright eyes of the tom-tit and the harvest-mouse.'

'That has the sound of something from one of your books,' she declared, scornfully. 'That is not life.' And with a sob she turned and ran from him.

13

Oh, who art thou, so swiftly flying?
My name is Love, the child replied,
Swifter I pass than south winds sighing.
Thomas Love Peacock.

Winter was a time of cosy luxury for Dolly. There was no need for her to do anything to cause her the least discomfort. She could sit by a blazing fire all day and read or sew. Or what? What else? She remembered her childhood at Marlipins, cold hands and chilblains, the cowhouse the warmest place, after her mother's kitchen, so that milking became one of the most popular chores.

Well, she had chosen money and boredom. For more than twenty years she had had nothing to do but enjoy herself, and somehow there had been little enjoyment in all that time. Only her brief love-affair with Peter Baker had shown her how much she had been missing in life.

If Peter had not returned, if she had not been given this second chance, she supposed she would have settled down to a middle-age of resignation. Why, she wondered, did she find it so difficult to come to a decision? Was it that she did not trust Peter? He had no money, and never would have; that was his easy-going, improvident way. He was depending on her getting an allowance from Christopher. But she didn't trust Christopher either. Probably he would be sufficiently crafty to wriggle out of supporting her and Benjy. In any case — and she smiled wryly — neither Christopher nor Peter wanted her for herself alone, as it was described in the romantic novels she read. Christopher had relinquished Marlipins to marry her, but that preference had long since been reversed. Now it seemed to her that she meant no more to him than the furnishings of the house and the staff that maintained them. I'm a kind of old retainer, she decided.

Why not go with Peter, then, and take a chance? It was the thought of Benjy which made her hesitate, or, rather, of Benjy and Tom, for who could contemplate separating them?

She had talked to Tom, hoping he might say something to help her to decide.

'Have you made up your mind, Tom, about what you want to do? It's almost five months since you left school.'

'Oh, my mind's made up all right, but I can't do much about it.' He sounded depressed.

'Why not?'

'You know what I want to be, an electrical engineer, but Father won't allow it. It's the wretched stables. I hate racehorses.' His voice rose to a passionate intensity, which was rare for Tom.

'If you feel so strongly you must take matters into your own hands. You're a grown man. Go to London, to one of the engineering firms. You've had a good education. I'm sure you'd get a job. I haven't much money, but I can let you have a little, just to tide you over.'

He looked down at his interlocked fingers. 'Thank you.' He could not bring himself to call her 'Mother.' 'Thank you, but I couldn't do that.'

'You must. You must make an effort.'

'There's Benjy.'

'Are you going to be a nursemaid to your brother all your life?' She spoke angrily, because she was sorry for the boy, and because she felt he was influencing her against taking Benjy and going to Peter. 'Benjy has me.'

Tom had no false modesty concerning his importance to Benjy. 'That's not the same.'

'Well, you certainly can't hang around here for ever, pushing a wheel-chair through the gardens. You'll get fat and lazy.'

The conversation had not really settled anything, so a few days later she took the train to Heathfield and went to the house where Peter lodged.

He had a small back room in a dingy Victorian cottage, and the owner, a widow, did not greet Dolly with any enthusiasm, which caused her to wonder whether Peter had been paying his rent regularly.

'I was afraid you might be out at work,' she said to him.

'No, there's hardly any work available on the land in December, as you should know, but maybe you've forgotten. You've been lying on a feather-bed so long.'

'And you've been shenanecking round the world long enough to have made a fortune,' Dolly retorted.

Peter laughed. 'I'm not interested in money.'

'No, not when you have to work for it. But remember I was the third benefit when you asked me to leave Christopher. The good income came before me.'

'Before or after, what does it matter?'

'You really want me, don't you, Peter?'

'Of course! No other woman has ever appealed to me like you do. I get hungry for you. Come on!' He pulled her to the bed, pushed her down on it. 'Lovely body!'

Expertly he began to undress her. 'I bet Christopher doesn't give you much now. Does he ever try?'

She pushed his hands away. 'Wait, Peter!'

'Wait? Why should I? This is what you came for, isn't it?'

'I want to talk to you.'

'We can talk after.'

'No. Listen!'

He was stroking her, caressing her as only he could do. She felt herself weakening, but fought against it.

'Peter, I think Christopher is in trouble.'

She had his full attention then. He took his hands away. 'What kind of trouble?'

'Financial. He is betting heavily.'

'Pooh! What's a little gamble for a man with his money?'

'When he gets home from the races he is almost always in a bad temper. Bills have been coming in. I've watched his face as he opens them. You know what he's like when he's in a temper. I'm afraid of him.'

'That's nothing new. Can't understand why you didn't leave him years ago.'

'Mr Cruttenden, the trainer, has been to the house several times to see him, and the servants are not nearly so respectful as they used to be.'

Peter's eyes narrowed. 'What are you trying to tell me?'

'Only that I don't think we can depend on getting a large allowance from Christopher.'

'As long as he's got it he'll have to pay.'

'I'm not sure, not in his present mood. He might rate his money higher than his pride. Supposing he should swear on oath that Benjy was not his son? Then he would owe us nothing.'

Peter looked thoughtful. 'That could be.'

Dolly took a deep breath. 'So you see how matters stand. But it needn't make any difference to us or to Benjy. I don't think I can endure it up there at Farncombes much longer. The sooner I can get away, the better. Shall I take the plunge, Peter?'

He stared at her. 'What? Now?'

'Why not?'

'In the winter? Getting on for Christmas? What should we use for money?'

'You've just said you're not interested in money.'

'Being uninterested and starving are two different things,' he told her, scornfully.

Dolly sighed. She wished Peter were a little more romantic. When she was younger it had not seemed to matter. She had been hungry for admiration, hungry for sex. But now she would have been grateful for a touch of tenderness. She wished also that she had not put any doubts into his mind concerning the probability of getting money from Christopher. Somehow she would force Christopher to make her an allowance, even if it meant taking Benjy and keeping out of Peter's way for a while, so that Christopher could not claim she had left him for another man. As for the betting, that was nothing to worry about. Christopher had the Farncombe estate, and the great house which must be worth a fortune.

She smiled at Peter. 'We shall not starve.'

He glanced at her suspiciously. 'Changed your tune suddenly, haven't you? What's the idea?'

'You know perfectly well. A woman doesn't care to be married for her money, any more than a man does.'

'There was a time when a woman took a dowry with her.'

She lost patience with him. 'Oh, stop talking about money! I thought, when you came back, you'd be different.'

'I am different. I'm older, I'm going bald, and there are wrinkles coming on your face.'

'I think you are a beast.'

She was angry and dissatisfied when she left him. Could she really endure living with him? Would he be kind to Benjy? Taking everything into consideration, there was little to choose between him and Christopher, she thought, miserably. Why had she been so unlucky in her choice of men? But had there been any choice for her? She had married Christopher to save Marlipins, and Christopher had thrown Peter across her path when he engaged him as farm manager. Now, in her mood of depression, she felt she wanted neither of them.

Restlessly she wandered around the house, which was gloomy in the dark days of winter, despite its expensive, ornate furniture. Spring was a long way off, but what would spring bring her, except summer, and then another winter?

By the following morning the skies had cleared, and Tom carried Benjy downstairs and settled him in his wheel-chair.

'We'll have a good long walk,' Tom said. He would have liked to stride out, use some of his pent-up energy, but ever since the day when they had met Daisy and he had raced back across the fields, Benjy had been nervous of being pushed at any more than the most decorous speed.

They went down the main drive which was planted with young beech-trees. In Christopher's imagination this was a venerable

228

avenue with smooth, soaring trunks like cathedral pillars, but at present they were no more than ambitious saplings some ten feet high. The low winter sun shining through the tracery of branches still held some warmth. It was a pleasant day, Tom thought, marred only by the fact that Benjy was sitting instead of walking or running beside him.

The drive was long and straight, so that they could see from some distance the figure approaching them.

'Who's that?' Benjy asked.

Tom recognised the man as he drew nearer. 'It's that fellow with the funny name who came to luncheon.'

'Clay — ' Benjy remembered ' — Clayton.'

'Slyfield,' Tom capped it.

Peter's pace quickened until he stopped by the wheel-chair. 'Hullo, you boys!'

'Hullo, sir!' Whether they liked him or not, their manners were impeccable. 'Are you on your way to the house?' Tom asked.

'Yes, I have a letter for your mother.'

'She's at home, so you'll be able to see her.'

'Well, I'm in a hurry. A letter will be better. It will explain everything.'

Tom waited politely, and Peter took a step, then stopped, as if an idea had occurred to him. 'I was going to give this to one of the servants, but it would save time if — would it be too much trouble, old chap, to run back to the house and give it to your mother?'

'Oh, no, sir! No trouble at all.'

'Are you sure? That's splendid. Your legs are younger than mine. I'll stay with Benjy until you get back.'

Even though Tom ran, it seemed to Peter that it was a considerable time before he was out of sight. He stood with what patience he could muster, but the moment the boy disappeared, he went into action. He grasped the handle of the chair and continued down the drive, breaking into a run.

'What are you doing?' Benjy demanded. 'Where are we going?'

Peter did not trouble to answer. Contemplating the remaining length of the drive he realised he would not be out of sight before Tom re-appeared.

'We've got to wait for Tom,' Benjy insisted.

There was only one thing to do. Peter jerked the chair round at right angles and heaved it up on to the grass. Maybe he could be beyond the trees and in the shelter of the thick shrubbery ahead.

'Stop!' Benjy implored. 'Please stop!'

Peter put on more speed. The chair bumped and leapt. Benjy was reminded of that nightmare journey across the fields. He began to scream.

'Shut up!' Peter commanded.

Benjy ignored him.

Peter stopped, went round the chair and held his fist close to Benjy's face. 'If you make another sound — ' He spoke quietly, but there was no mistaking his intention. 'If you make another sound, even a whimper, I'll break your bloody jaw.'

14

Dame Fortune is a fickle gipsy,
And always blind, and often tipsy.
                    Winthrop Mackworth Praed.

The house was rambling, product of an architect who believed Australians possessed no yardsticks and measured only in miles. There were too many corridors, and it was several minutes before Tom tracked Dolly down.

He was out of breath. 'This — this is for you.'

'What is it?' She did not bother to reach out, so he thrust it into her hand. 'It's from — from that man — Clayton Slyfield.'

She frowned. 'Who?' For she had forgotten the silly name Peter had invented.

Paper-knives — some silver, some ivory — were a part of the equipment of the house, but Dolly did not bother to fetch one. She tore open the envelope with her fingers, conscious of a small twinge of apprehension. Only something urgent could have caused Peter to send a letter here.

As she read it Tom watched her face

becoming deathly pale. He thought she would faint, and wished he knew the proper procedure for revival. But she put her hand on the back of a chair to support herself and took a deep breath.

'Tom, where did you leave Benjy?'

'In the drive.'

She stumbled to the window, looked out, but there was no one in sight. 'Run as fast as you can, find him, and don't let him out of your sight.'

'But — '

'Don't talk! Go! Hurry!'

She followed as quickly as she could, knowing she could never catch Tom, but praying he would be in time.

Halfway down the drive she stopped, exhausted.

On a beech branch a robin sat chirruping gently. There was no other sound. The winter morning was calm and peaceful and empty.

Far in the distance Tom came into view, and he was alone. Impatiently Dolly went towards him, unable to wait, though she could not hope he would have anything to tell her.

'Well?' she demanded.

He shook his head. 'I went right down to the gates. There's no one, no sign of anyone.'

He paused, then asked, 'Mother — ' He had not intended to call her that any more, but habit from babyhood came naturally at such a moment.

'Mother, where is Benjy? What has happened?'

'Peter has taken him.'

'Peter?'

'Yes, that's his real name. He was your father's bailiff. Now he has kidnapped Benjy.'

Tom's mouth opened. 'Kidnapped? What for?'

'Money, of course. What else?'

'But how did he know?' Tom sounded bewildered. 'How did he know that he would meet us, that he should have the letter ready?'

'I told him you took Benjy out each morning for a walk in the grounds. I was a fool. I should have sent him packing. I knew what he was like.'

Slowly they walked back up the drive towards the house. Tom felt at a loss. This was a man's job, and it made him realise he was scarcely more than a boy. 'Should we tell the police?'

Dolly tried to consider the consequences. An arrest. A trial. What kind of mud would Peter stir up from the past? 'We'd better leave it to your father to decide.'

'But Father will pay the man. He'll give him the money to get Benjy back.' Tom tried to sound confident, but his voice shook, and both sentences became questions.

'Five thousand pounds?' Dolly saw the horror on Tom's face, and wished she had not spoken. 'Oh, I suppose he'll do it,' she said, hurriedly. 'We must wait and see.'

The waiting was not as long as usual. Christopher returned early. He did not go into any of the downstairs rooms, but crossed the hall and began to ascend the stairs. Dolly heard him, and ran to the foot of the staircase. 'Christopher!'

He turned. 'What is it?'

The dimness of the hall prevented her from seeing that his face was livid, and that he put his hand on the banister to steady himself.

'Please come into the drawing-room. I want to talk to you.'

'Can't it wait?'

'No. I'm sorry. It's urgent.'

Reluctantly he came down. Tom sprang to his feet as they entered the room. He was desperately anxious to take some action, to learn what Christopher proposed to do, but Dolly said, 'Please leave us alone, Tom. I wish to speak to your father in private.' It cost her an effort to say this, for she knew too well Christopher's tendency to violence, and she would have welcomed Tom's protection, but she felt it cruel to expose him to a scene which might shame and embarrass him.

Tom hesitated. 'Must I go?'

'Yes, please.'

She clenched her hands as he went, resisting the impulse to change her mind.

Christopher stood with his back to the fire, legs straddled. 'Well? What have you done now?'

'It's Benjy. He — he has disappeared.'

'Oh, yes? I suppose he's got up out of his chair and run away.'

She found she could not give him the news, could not put it into words, so she handed him the letter, silently, and went and stood by the window, unable to watch his face. She did not hear him moving on the thick carpet, did not know he was behind her until she felt her wrist grasped. At arm's length he pulled her towards him, then flung her across the room. By a miracle she missed the fireplace and the heavy marble surround, and crashed to the floor against nothing more lethal than a side-table, spilling the porcelain ornaments upon it.

Slowly she pulled herself to her feet. She had bumped her head, and her hand was bleeding from a piece of a broken bowl, but she was not seriously hurt.

Christopher was shouting at her. 'So that is what you have been doing behind my back, you dirty little harlot. Couldn't leave your fancy man alone, even after all these years. But how did he find you now? Not so nice, I warrant. Any shrivelled old bed-fagot would have done him as well.'

Only vaguely did she hear Christopher as he continued to revile her, using words he had picked up in his youth from the vagabonds of the outback, and more recently from the riffraff of the racecourse. She pressed her handkerchief against the cut and waited for him to finish.

'You will give Peter the money, won't you?' she asked, quietly.

Christopher laughed.

'I'm afraid for Benjy's safety,' she added.

'Pay? Pay good money, five thousand pounds, for a puny little cripple who is nothing but a liability? You've told me often enough he's not my son — '

'I don't know, Christopher. How could I be absolutely sure?'

'Oho! So you'd father him on me when it suits you. Well, I've had enough of you, and of the kid. I've finished with you. Let the bastard keep his little bastard.'

'Christopher, this is the last thing I'll ask of you. I don't want anything for myself.'

'Just as well, considering you won't get anything. Now I've a piece of news for you. I've had bad luck. They let me down, those horses did, and I've finally lost the lot. D'you hear what I say? I'm ruined, bankrupt, broke. Don't look so blank, woman! Have you nothing to say?'

'I — I'm sorry. But it can't be so terribly bad. I mean, you still have the land, and this house, and the stables. You told me the horses are worth a fortune.'

Again Christopher laughed. 'That's good! That's rich, that is! You've no conception what gambling really is. It's increasing your bets, and doubling up, and knowing your luck will change — only it doesn't. Let me tell you, this house and the land and the stables wouldn't begin to pay my debts, not even if I stripped it down to the clothes on my back. So, you see, your lover can whistle for his money. I'll make him a present of Benjy instead. But one thing I will do — '

Dolly shrank away as he walked towards her, but he appeared not to notice her. He was smiling. 'I'll not have that lecher cuckold me for the second time. I'm going to him, and I'm going to beat the life out of him.'

'No! No, you mustn't do that.'

'Why not? Are you afraid I'll spoil him for

you? Well, when I've finished with him he'll never show his face around here again, 'cos it won't be worth showing.'

'It won't do any good, Christopher. Violence can't help. Let me persuade Peter to bring Benjy back. I'm sure he will. When he learns there's no money — '

'Where can I find him? Where's he living?'

Dolly's mouth was dry with fear. She knew she should not give Christopher Peter's address, because in his present mood he was likely to do something desperate and irrevocable.

While she hesitated, trying to moisten her lips, he went towards her. Memories of his past assaults flashed before her, of his uncontrollable attacks, not sparing her even in her pregnancy. Now he was like a madman, driven by his financial ruin in addition to his vicious temper.

She screamed before his fingers closed round her throat, and that was when Tom rushed in. He had been lingering uneasily in the hall, hearing Christopher's raised voice, though the words did not penetrate the heavy door. He was loth to interrupt, but Dolly's cry put an end to his doubts. He scarcely noticed the overturned table and the broken ornaments, for it seemed to him that murder was being done.

He flew at Christopher, dragging him away. It was not easy, but Tom was a strong young man. He saw Dolly slide to the ground, half choking, and then Christopher was turning on him, wild, red-eyed. Tom did the only thing that seemed possible. He put his hands on Christopher's chest and pushed him roughly.

It was intended as no more than a deterrent, but Christopher happened to step on a piece of china, stumbled, lost his balance, and crashed to the floor, where he lay motionless.

Tom thought, 'Oh, God, I have killed him!'

Dolly was sitting crying weakly. He lifted her into a chair and then went for help. One of the servants was sent for the doctor and another assisted Tom to carry Christopher to his bed.

To Tom's relief Christopher was not dead. There was a cut on his head and his breathing was heavy and unnatural, but at least he was alive.

Tom went back to Dolly. She was still shocked and her throat was giving her pain. She did not ask about Christopher's condition.

'I shouldn't have done it,' Tom said, miserably. 'I shouldn't have been so violent.'

Dolly began to laugh, then stopped when it hurt her. 'You? Violent?' Her voice was hoarse.

'I thought he was going to — '

'I know. He might have done. When he's angry — '

'I can't help feeling guilty.'

'You probably saved my life.'

'Yes, but — '

In a remarkably short time the doctor arrived, and the doctor was Tirell.

'You!' Dolly exclaimed.

'Have you any objection?' Tirell asked, gravely.

'Oh, no! It's just that I didn't expect you.'

'Your man had the sense to fetch me. Maybe he did not know you had no communication with Marlipins.'

'Tirell, that wasn't what I wanted.'

'I realise it. Now may I see my patient?'

Dolly and Tom waited in the drawing-room. Mechanically Tom righted the overturned table and pushed aside some of the wrecked ornaments. When he heard footsteps on the stairs he went to the door. His legs felt weak with fear, but as he looked over his shoulder at Dolly she seemed calm.

Tirell entered the room and Tom closed the door. Dolly said nothing and it was Tom who had to ask, 'How is he?'

Tirell was frowning. This was the kind of news she was always sorry to give. 'I'm afraid there is not much hope of his recovery.'

Tom's heart sank. Would he have to endure for the rest of his life this burden of responsibility? 'I didn't mean to hurt him, but I had to stop him. He was going to — '

Tirell had been watching Dolly. Now she looked at Tom in surprise. 'What did you do?'

'I pushed him, and he fell.'

'Oh, that was not the trouble. The head wound is nothing. He has had a stroke, a massive brain haemorrhage. It has probably been building up for some time. Anything could have brought it on, perhaps violent emotion.'

The weight slid from Tom. He felt light as air, then reproached himself for feeling joy at such a time.

Tirell turned to Dolly. 'I think you should go to Christopher and stay with him. He may not regain consciousness, but if he should — ' Tirell hesitated before finishing. 'He may need you.'

Shakily Dolly rose to her feet and went to the writing-desk which held her correspondence. 'Tom, I want you to ride over to Heathfield. Here is the address. Tell Peter Baker he can bring Benjy back.' She paused, feeling there was something else she must say, and added, 'Tell him also that there is no money.'

15

Though I am somewhat aged,
Yet is not love assuaged.

Robert Jones.

Christopher died during the night.

Hour after hour Dolly had sat beside him. There was a kind of peace in the room. Maybe, she thought, it was because Christopher was quiet at last, no longer driven by the urgency of his desires, desire for Marlipins, desire for sons.

There was only one interruption. Tom came to say Benjy was home again. She nodded and he went away. There was no need to ask whether Peter had gone. She knew he would have done. There was nothing now for him at Farncombes.

At two-thirty Christopher had opened his eyes. Dolly gave a little start of fear. Often she had had the feeling that he could read her mind.

He mumbled something. She leaned closer, but could not understand him. He was almost completely paralysed, yet she could sense the tremendous effort he was making.

'What is it?' she asked. 'What are you trying to tell me?'

He glared at her, and his expression said silently, 'Don't ask damfool questions!'

At last his mouth formed a word which came out clearly, triumphantly, 'Debbie.'

She was surprised. What message could he possibly have for Debbie?

'Tell Debbie.' He took a shallow, painful breath. 'Sterile. Always. No children.'

She guessed he must have intended to say 'Dolly.' Evidently he was confused. But his eyes still held hers. 'Debbie,' he repeated. 'Promise.'

Those were the last words he spoke. He seemed to be sleeping, but later she realised that he had sunk into a coma. When Tirell arrived very early in the morning Dolly had not moved from her place.

'He has gone,' Tirell said, gently. 'I think you should rest now.'

Stiffly Dolly rose to her feet. 'I'm not tired. Please leave it to me to tell the boys.'

She went to her room and bathed and dressed, and reckoned that by then the boys would be up.

They were in the breakfast-room, Benjy in his wheel-chair, neat and tidy, shaved and brushed and combed. Dolly felt a surge of gratitude towards Tom. Who else would ever offer Benjy such tender care?

She went to Benjy and kissed him. 'Are you all right, dear?'

'Yes, thank you, Mother.'

'He — Peter — he didn't harm you?'

'No. He took me to his lodgings, and he talked a lot. He's really quite a decent chap, you know.'

Dolly turned away to hide the smile she could not repress. Few must be the times when Peter was described in such terms.

It was Tom who thought of the man upstairs. 'How is — ' He did not want to say it, but he had no other word. 'How is Father?'

Dolly too had difficulty in finding a word. She murmured, 'He has passed on,' then despised herself for the trite euphemism. 'He — he didn't suffer. He just went to sleep.' She wanted to spare Benjy some of the grief she expected from him. Tom was all right; he had never loved Christopher.

She glanced at Benjy, ready to put her arms about him, to try to comfort him, but Benjy's expression was one of astonishment. It was as though he found Christopher's death beyond credibility. She put out her hand, fearing hysteria, but what actually happened left her stupefied.

Slowly, Benjy stood up, his hands pressing

on the arms of the chair. Then he took a step forward, and another. He had taken three steps before he wavered, swayed, and Tom caught him and helped him back.

Dolly knelt beside him. 'Oh, Benjy! You can stand. You can walk. That's wonderful!'

'I know,' he agreed, without emotion.

'But how long — have you tried before?'

'Yes. I often try, when no one's looking.'

'Darling, I'm so glad. We had almost given up hope. Now we can send for those doctors from London. They can prescribe treatment, give you special exercises — We'll get you quite well. Oh, it was cruel to keep it from us. You should have told Tom and me.'

Benjy shook his head. 'I couldn't. I couldn't let Father find out.'

'Whyever not? If only he had known before — '

'I couldn't,' Benjy repeated. 'He'd have wanted me to ride that horse.'

'Silly boy! You could have refused.'

'I couldn't.' It seemed as though he had to repeat those words. 'He would have been disappointed, and angry with me. So long as I didn't walk I was safe.'

The news of what was looked upon as Benjy's miracle almost eclipsed that of Christopher's bankruptcy and death, and when, after the funeral, the house was put up for sale, the villagers wagged their heads knowingly. That was the way it was, they said, when foreigners came in and acted like they owned the whole of the Sussex Weald. Christopher Waldron had never really belonged, but now young Dolly was back with her family, things would be on an even keel again.

Dolly asked her mother, 'Can you really take me and the boys? Won't it be too much for you?'

Alice beamed. 'This is the brightest day I've known for years. Too much? Too much to have my four children around me?'

'Three of us widowed,' Dolly said, soberly.

Alice refused to be anything but cheerful. 'There's worse things than that, though I grant you a widow-man is a sadder sight than a widow-woman. I wish Joe-Ben — '

Joe-Ben was, like his mother, given to counting his blessings. He was a lucky one, wasn't he, with a successful career and a harmonious family, and a daughter of his own?

Daisy was getting on splendidly as a teacher, and the school was prospering. Debbie even considered taking on another assistant. 'Would you like to help me, Dolly?'

Dolly was not sure. 'You were always the

clever one. I think I'd rather help Rose with the farm.'

Debbie laughed. 'What help does he need, with all that machinery?'

Dolly looked speculatively at her twin. It was marvellous for them to be together again, friends as before, though there were one or two things she did not understand. Why, for instance, when she gave Debbie Christopher's last message, had Debbie been silent for a moment or two, and then said nothing more than, 'Thank God!'

She did not understand Joe-Ben either. Debbie told her about the French girl, Daisy's friend. 'She got on so well with Joe-Ben, but of course she was years too young for him.'

'Where is she now?'

'Oh, she's studying art in Paris. I don't suppose we'll hear from her again.'

A few weeks later, however, Daisy received a letter, which she took to her father. 'I've heard from Alix.'

'Oh?'

She almost went away without saying any more, because he sounded utterly uninterested, but a streak of obstinacy made her persist. 'She will have a holiday in the spring.'

He did not reply, and in the past that

would have been the end of it. She would have left frustrated and miserable, convinced that her father cared nothing for her. Perhaps she would have sought out her grandmother and asked her, 'Why was I born?'

Alice knew the answer to that question. 'Because your father and mother loved one another.'

'Then why doesn't he love me?'

'I'm sure he does.'

Sensitive child as she was, Daisy never failed to catch the doubt in her grandmother's voice. But now things were different. Her work as a schoolteacher had given her confidence. Her father, she thought, was like the occasional difficult children with whom she had to contend. They were not stupid; they simply erected a barrier around themselves.

'Alix would like to spend her holidays here.'

She had Joe-Ben's attention. He turned sharply and looked at her.

'Oh, no! No, that wouldn't be convenient.'

'What do you mean, convenient? There's plenty of room in the house. She wouldn't be in your way.'

'She would. She interferes with my work. And there's your grandmother to consider. She's not as young as she was, and the extra cooking and so on — ' His voice tailed off as he ran out of excuses.

Anger built up in Daisy. It was as if it had been growing with her throughout her childhood, watered by the tears she sometimes shed alone in bed. 'You are a detestable creature,' she told him, hotly. 'You don't care for anybody or anything except your beastly birds and mice and insects and plants. You don't belong to this family. Why don't you go and live in a cave like a proper hermit?'

He stared at her, amazed at her outburst, and then he too lost his temper. 'How dare you talk to me like that! I am your father.'

She stuck her nose in the air. 'No one would notice it.'

'If you were younger I would smack you and send you to bed.'

'No, you wouldn't. You'd pack me off to an expensive school, to be rid of me.'

'At this moment you are no credit to it.'

'I am saying what I think.'

'Then I will do the same. I think you are without gratitude, unworthy of the sacrifice I made for you.'

'Sacrifice?' There was contempt in her voice. 'What did you ever sacrifice for me?'

'Alix.'

'Alix? What do you mean?'

'You wouldn't understand,' he told her, impatiently. 'I love Alix, and that is why she must not come here again.'

'You love her?'

'Is that so strange? Has it never entered your head that I am human?'

'But where do I come into it? What is this sacrifice?'

He sighed. His resentment died down, and he was embarrassed that he had revealed himself. 'I know I've not been much of a father, but this one thing I could do for you. I could at least put you first, restrain myself from giving you a step-mother of your own age.'

She blinked, and then her eyes widened. 'You mean you thought I should be jealous?'

'That would be understandable.'

'She loves you,' Daisy said.

Joe-Ben looked down. 'I can't think why.'

Daisy sniffed. 'Madame de Valmore condemned false modesty. Actually you are a very handsome man.' She paused, then added, 'for your age.'

'Thank you,' Joe-Ben murmured, awkwardly.

'Is Alix important to you?'

'The most important person in my life.'

'And you gave her up for me.'

Joe-Ben waited nervously. He feared Daisy might fling herself weeping into his arms, and then he would not know what to do. Sentiment did not come easily to him now. He was out of practice.

But she only smiled and nodded. 'Well, that's all right,' she said, brisky, 'and I can tell you there's nothing I'd like better than for you and Alix to marry.'

Joe-Ben doubted the message his ears received. 'Do you mean it?'

'Well, of course! It's a marvellous idea. I've worked it all out.' She spoke with unusual enthusiasm, and suddenly there seemed to move in her a touch of the wild Joan. 'She won't be my step-mother,' she went on, 'she'll be my sister, but I shall call her my half-sister when I introduce her, otherwise people would think you were her father.' She looked sideways at him, and added, primly, 'One has to avoid embarrassment when there is disparity in ages.'

'Of course!' Joe-Ben agreed.

'So shall I write and invite her?'

'No!'

He did not wait to see her stunned expression. He was bounding up the stairs to his bedroom. Dolly heard him, and followed, wondering what was the cause of all the noise.

She looked in through the open door. On the bed was a Gladstone bag, into which he was stuffing various objects.

'What on earth are you doing?'

'Packing.'

'I can see that. But where are you going?'

He spared time to flash her a smile. 'To Paris, of course!' And then he snapped the bag shut.

THE END

Other titles in the
Ulverscroft Large Print Series:

THE GREENWAY
Jane Adams
When Cassie and her twelve-year-old cousin Suzie had taken a short cut through an ancient Norfolk pathway, Suzie had simply vanished . . . Twenty years on, Cassie is still tormented by nightmares. She returns to Norfolk, determined to solve the mystery.

FORTY YEARS
ON THE WILD FRONTIER
Carl Breihan & W. Montgomery
Noted Western historian Carl Breihan has culled from the handwritten diaries of John Montgomery, grandfather of co-author Wayne Montgomery, new facts about Wyatt Earp, Doc Holliday, Bat Masterson and other famous and infamous men and women who gained notoriety when the Western Frontier was opened up.

TAKE NOW, PAY LATER
Joanna Dessau
This fiction based on fact is the love-turning-to-hate story of Robert Carr, Earl of Somerset, and his wife, Frances.

McLEAN AT THE GOLDEN OWL
George Goodchild
Inspector McLean has resigned from Scotland Yard's CID and has opened an office in Wimpole Street. With the help of his able assistant, Tiny, he solves many crimes, including those of kidnapping, murder and poisoning.

KATE WEATHERBY
Anne Goring
Derbyshire, 1849: The Hunter family are the arrogant, powerful masters of Clough Grange. Their feuds are sparked by a generation of guilt, despair and ill-fortune. But their passions are awakened by the arrival of nineteen-year-old Kate Weatherby.

A VENETIAN RECKONING
Donna Leon
When the body of a prominent international lawyer is found in the carriage of an intercity train, Commissario Guido Brunetti begins to dig deeper into the secret lives of the once great and good.

A TASTE FOR DEATH
Peter O'Donnell

Modesty Blaise and Willie Garvin take on impossible odds in the shape of Simon Delicata, the man with a taste for death, and Swordmaster, Wenczel, in a terrifying duel. Finally, in the Sahara desert, the intrepid pair must summon every killing skill to survive.

SEVEN DAYS FROM MIDNIGHT
Rona Randall

In the Comet Theatre, London, seven people have good reason for wanting beautiful Maxine Culver out of the way. Each one has reason to fear her blackmail. But whose shadow is it that lurks in the wings, waiting to silence her once and for all?

QUEEN OF THE ELEPHANTS
Mark Shand

Mark Shand knows about the ways of elephants, but he is no match for the tiny Parbati Barua, the daughter of India's greatest expert on the Asian elephant, the late Prince of Gauripur, who taught her everything. Shand sought out Parbati to take part in a film about the plight of the wild herds today in north-east India.

THE DARKENING LEAF
Caroline Stickland

On storm-tossed Chesil Bank in 1847, the young lovers, Philobeth and Frederick, prevent wreckers mutilating the apparent corpse of a young woman. Discovering she is still alive, Frederick takes her to his grandmother's home. But the rescue is to have violent and far-reaching effects . . .

A WOMAN'S TOUCH
Emma Stirling

When Fenn went to stay on her uncle's farm in Africa, the lovely Helena Starr seemed to resent her — especially when Dr Jason Kemp agreed to Fenn helping in his bush hospital. Though it seemed Jason saw Fenn as little more than a child, her feelings for him were those of a woman.

A DEAD GIVEAWAY
Various Authors

This book offers the perfect opportunity to sample the skills of five of the finest writers of crime fiction — Clare Curzon, Gillian Linscott, Peter Lovesey, Dorothy Simpson and Margaret Yorke.

DOUBLE INDEMNITY — MURDER FOR INSURANCE
Jad Adams

This is a collection of true cases of murderers who insured their victims then killed them — or attempted to. Each tense, compelling account tells a story of cold-blooded plotting and elaborate deception.

THE PEARLS OF COROMANDEL
By Keron Bhattacharya

John Sugden, an ambitious young Oxford graduate, joins the Indian Civil Service in the early 1920s and goes to uphold the British Raj. But he falls in love with a young Hindu girl and finds his loyalties tragically divided.

WHITE HARVEST
Louis Charbonneau

Kathy McNeely, a marine biologist, sets out for Alaska to carry out important research. But when she stumbles upon an illegal ivory poaching operation that is threatening the world's walrus population, she soon realises that she will have to survive more than the harsh elements . . .

TO THE GARDEN ALONE
Eve Ebbett

Widow Frances Morley's short, happy marriage was childless, and in a succession of borders she attempts to build a substitute relationship for the husband and family she does not have. Over all hovers the shadow of the man who terrorized her childhood.

CONTRASTS
Rowan Edwards

Julia had her life beautifully planned — she was building a thriving pottery business as well as sharing her home with her friend Pippa, and having fun owning a goat. But the goat's problems brought the new local vet, Sebastian Trent, into their lives.

MY OLD MAN AND THE SEA
David and Daniel Hays

Some fathers and sons go fishing together. David and Daniel Hays decided to sail a tiny boat seventeen thousand miles to the bottom of the world and back. Together, they weave a story of travel, adventure, and difficult, sometimes terrifying, sailing.

SQUEAKY CLEAN
James Pattinson
An important attribute of a prospective candidate for the United States presidency is not to have any dirt in your background which an eager muckraker can dig up. Senator William S. Gallicauder appeared to fit the bill perfectly. But then a skeleton came rattling out of an English cupboard.

NIGHT MOVES
Alan Scholefield
It was the first case that Macrae and Silver had worked on together. Malcolm Underdown had brutally stabbed to death Edward Craig and had attempted to murder Craig's fiancée, Jane Harrison. He swore he would be back for her. Now, four years later, he has simply walked from the mental hospital. Macrae and Silver must get to him — before he gets to Jane.

GREATEST CAT STORIES
Various Authors
Each story in this collection is chosen to show the cat at its best. James Herriot relates a tale about two of his cats. Stella Whitelaw has written a very funny story about a lion. Other stories provide examples of courageous, clever and lucky cats.

THE HAND OF DEATH
Margaret Yorke

The woman had been raped and murdered. As the police pursue their relentless inquiries, decent, gentle George Fortescue, the typical man-next-door, finds himself accused. While the real killer serenely selects his third victim — and then his fourth . . .

VOW OF FIDELITY
Veronica Black

Sister Joan of the Daughters of Compassion is shocked to discover that three of her former fellow art college students have recently died violently. When another death occurs, Sister Joan realizes that she must pit her wits against a cunning and ruthless killer.

MARY'S CHILD
Irene Carr

Penniless and desperate, Chrissie struggles to support herself as the Victorian years give way to the First World War. Her childhood friends, Ted and Frank, fall hopelessly in love with her. But there is only one man Chrissie loves, and fate and one man bent on revenge are determined to prevent the match . . .

THE SWIFTEST EAGLE
Alice Dwyer-Joyce

This book moves from Scotland to Malaya — before British Raj and now — and then to war-torn Vietnam and Cambodia . . . Virginia meets Gareth casually in the Western Isles, with no inkling of the sacrifice he must make for her.

VICTORIA & ALBERT
Richard Hough

Victoria and Albert had nine children and the family became the archetype of the nineteenth century. But the relationship between the Queen and her Prince Consort was passionate and turbulent; thunderous rows threatened to tear them apart, but always reconciliation and love broke through.

BREEZE: WAIF OF THE WILD
Marie Kelly

Bernard and Marie Kelly swapped their lives in London for a remote farmhouse in Cumbria. But they were to undergo an even more drastic upheaval when a two-day-old fragile roe deer fawn arrived on their doorstep. The knowledge of how to care for her was learned through sleepless nights and anxiety-filled days.

DEAR LAURA
Jean Stubbs

In Victorian London, Mr Theodore Crozier, of Crozier's Toys, succumbed to three grains of morphine. Wimbledon hoped it was suicide — but murder was whispered. Out of the neat cupboards of the Croziers' respectable home tumbled skeleton after skeleton.

MOTHER LOVE
Judith Henry Wall

Karen Billingsly begins to suspect that her son, Chad, has done something unthinkable — something beyond her wildest fears or imaginings. Gradually the terrible truth unfolds, and Karen must decide just how far she should go to protect her son from justice.

JOURNEY TO GUYANA
Margaret Bacon

In celebration of the anniversary of the emancipation of the African slaves in Guyana, the author published an account of her two-year stay there in the 1960s, revealing some fascinating insights into the multi-racial society.

WEDDING NIGHT
Gary Devon

Young actress Callie McKenna believes that Malcolm Rhodes is the man of her dreams. But a dark secret long buried in Malcolm's past is about to turn Callie's passion into terror.

RALPH EDWARDS
OF LONESOME LAKE
Ed Gould

Best known for his almost single-handed rescue of the trumpeter swans from extinction in North America, Ralph Edwards relates other aspects of his long, varied life, including experiences with his missionary parents in India, as a telegraph operator in World War I, and his eventual return to Lonesome Lake.

NEVER FAR FROM NOWHERE
Andrea Levy

Olive and Vivien were born in London to Jamaican parents. Vivien's life becomes a chaotic mix of friendships, youth clubs, skinhead violence, discos and college. But Olive, three years older and her skin a shade darker, has a very different tale to tell . . .

THE UNICORN SUMMER
Rhona Martin

When Joanna Pengerran was a child, she escaped from her murderous stepfather and took refuge among the tinkers. Across her path blunders Angel, a fugitive from prejudice and superstition. It is a meeting destined to disrupt both their lives.

FAMILY REUNIONS
Connie Monk

Claudia and Teddy's three children are now married, and it is a time to draw closer together again, man and wife rather than mother and father. But then their daughter introduces Adrian into the family circle. Young and attractive, Adrian arouses excitement and passion in Claudia that she had never expected to feel again.

SHADOW OF THE MARY CELESTE
Richard Rees

In 1872, the sailing ship *Mary Celeste* left New York. Exactly one month later, she was found abandoned — but completely seaworthy — six hundred miles off the coast of Spain, with no sign of captain or crew. After years of exhaustive research Richard Rees has unravelled the mystery.